Story a Day

for every day
of the year

SPRING

The Rescuers stories in this book feature characters from
the Disney film suggested by the books by Margery Sharp,
The Rescuers and *Miss Bianca*, published by Little, Brown
& Company.

Walt Disney's
Story a Day

for every day
of the year

SPRING

GOLDEN PRESS · NEW YORK

Western Publishing Company, Inc.
Racine, Wisconsin

Contents

Introduction

Here's one of a fantastic new series of Walt Disney books that's guaranteed to make *every* day of the year extra special! There are four books in the series—one for spring, one for summer, one for autumn and one for winter. Each book contains a story for every day of the season, so if you read all four you will have a story a day all year round, including one for the special days, like Christmas Day. All the stories have been specially written for the series and feature favorite Disney characters in lots of exciting and entertaining new adventures. And if you like to laugh you'll even find jokes in the books too! The illustrations, like the stories, are brand new and are all in sparkling color.

For every child who can read these books will make a treasured gift, and toddlers will find that bedtime *every* night will be a special event, as they fall asleep listening to tales of Mickey, Donald, Goofy and their Disneyland friends.

March Madness

Minnie: "What's on television?"
Mickey: "Just a vase of flowers and some dust!"

T he March Hare, leaping about with the joys of spring, met his friend the Mad Hatter.

"It's March!" said the Hare. "Nice month for madness!"

"You can't be properly mad without a hat," sniffed the Hatter. "*I'm* mad—that's why I'm called the Mad Hatter. But you're not mad. You're just an overgrown rabbit."

"A *rabbit*!" The March Hare was scandalized. "Of course I'm not a rabbit! Look at my ears—*twice* as long!"

"M'm," mused the Hatter, "perhaps that's the trouble. I mean, the top of your head is all taken up with ears, isn't it? There's no head you could possibly put a hat on. Poor Hare!"

"I'm *not* poor Hare!" shouted the March Hare, jumping up and down furiously. "I'm happy Hare—lucky Hare—*March* Hare!"

"But you're not mad," insisted the Hatter.

"I am, I am!" shrieked March Hare. "I'm madder than you'll ever be!"

"We'll see about that," said the Hatter. "I'll go and find the Dormouse and he can decide which of us is maddest."

"Right!" agreed the March Hare, but as the Hatter ran

8

off he felt a little worried. What if he was just an ordinary hare after all? What a comedown! How everyone would laugh! He chewed a daffodil stalk thoughtfully. How could he wear a hat? He munched his way up the stalk, thinking, until he came to the daffodil flower. It was too pretty to eat. Suddenly he had a brilliant idea. The end of his ear would just fit into the daffodil's trumpet! He slipped it on, then picked another daffodil for the other ear.

The Mad Hatter came back with the Dormouse, but stopped when he saw the March Hare's flowery hat. "I give up," he groaned. "I never thought you'd be mad enough to try and make a hat! You *must* be madder than I!"

"Only mad hares wear hats," yawned the Dormouse—and fell asleep.

"I've won!" crowed the March Hare. And he capered across the meadow, as mad as a Hatter—or, of course, as a March Hare!

9

Eeyore's Party

2
March

Wart: "I keep thinking there are two of me."
Doctor: "Eh? Would you repeat that? And this time, don't both speak at once."

Christopher Robin had given Eeyore a big jar of lemonade powder. Eeyore was very pleased with it. "I'll have a party," he said to himself, "after my lunch-time nap."

Eeyore woke up feeling refreshed after his sleep. "Time for my party," he said. "Good." And he sat down to wait for everyone to come. He had forgotten, though, that he hadn't *asked* anyone to his party! Nobody knew about it. Eeyore waited and waited.

Meanwhile, other people were doing other things. Kanga was looking for some thread to mend Roo's bib, but she couldn't find any. "We'll go and see if Pooh has got some," she said. "Come on, Roo." And they went to Pooh's house. He said he didn't have any thread but he had some very nice honey. "The thing is," he said, "I don't know if this honey is nicer than the last lot. What do you think, Kanga?"

"I don't know," said Kanga. "Let's go and ask Piglet."

They all went to Piglet's house and found Piglet looking for acorns. He said he didn't have any thread and he didn't know about the honey and suggested they should go and see Rabbit.

"Hallo!" said Rabbit. "Can't stop—must see Owl. Important news." He rushed off, followed by Kanga, Roo, Pooh and Piglet. But Owl's house had a notice on the door saying 'GONE TO TIGGER'S'. At Tigger's house Owl was talking seriously. "Nice animals, Tigger, do not bounce," he was saying. Tigger looked very bored and when he saw everyone arriving he shouted, "How nice to see you! Come in!"

But Tigger didn't have any thread and he didn't know about honey, and Rabbit had forgotten the important news he had to tell Owl. So they all went to see Eeyore . . .

"You're late," said Eeyore gloomily. "But never mind."

"Lemonade!" shouted Rabbit. "That was my important news! Christopher Robin gave Eeyore—"

"Have some lemonade," said Eeyore.

And they all drank lemonade and ate Pooh's honey and forgot about Kanga's thread and had a lovely party. *Especially* Eeyore!

The Digger

Busy Mickey Mouse was planting seeds. Lazy Pluto lay outside the back door, gnawing a juicy bone.

"I have baked a cake for you, Mickey!" called Minnie across the garden.

"Good!" beamed Mickey. "Gardening makes me hungry."

Mickey went indoors, and Pluto chewed the last piece of meat off his bone. Of course, the bone was still good for gnawing, and Pluto didn't want Minnie to throw it in the trash can. He must bury it with his other bones. "Mmm!" wondered Pluto. "But WHERE did I bury those bones? Er—let me see . . ."

When Mickey came out again he was horrified. His flowerbed was wrecked. There were big holes where his neat seed labels had been placed.

Pluto, at last, had found his boney treasure trove, and was kicking up earth as he buried his new bone with the others. Mickey's howls of rage brought Minnie running out of the house.

"What's the matter, Mickey?" she cried.

"Look what Pluto has done! He's dug up all the seeds I planted!" Mickey glowered at Pluto. Pluto was puzzled. All he'd done was bury his bone! However, he knew Mickey was cross with him and he slunk under the garden seat, feeling very sad.

"Cheer up, you two," smiled Minnie. "I'll go and buy some more seeds." So Minnie came back with some gaily-colored seed packets. "It's no use planting them," grunted Mickey, gloomily. "Pluto will just dig them up again." Minnie smiled mysteriously. "Pluto won't dig them up this time," she said.

Mickey planted the seeds and tied the packets to small sticks, so that he would know where each kind of flower was growing. Then, on the fence behind Pluto's bone-burying plot, Minnie pinned a drawing of a large BONE! She called Pluto to look at the picture. He wagged his tail and licked his lips.

"There!!" chuckled Minnie. "Pluto will know where his bones are buried now. He won't dig up YOUR seeds again, Mickey!"

Caught in her Own Net!

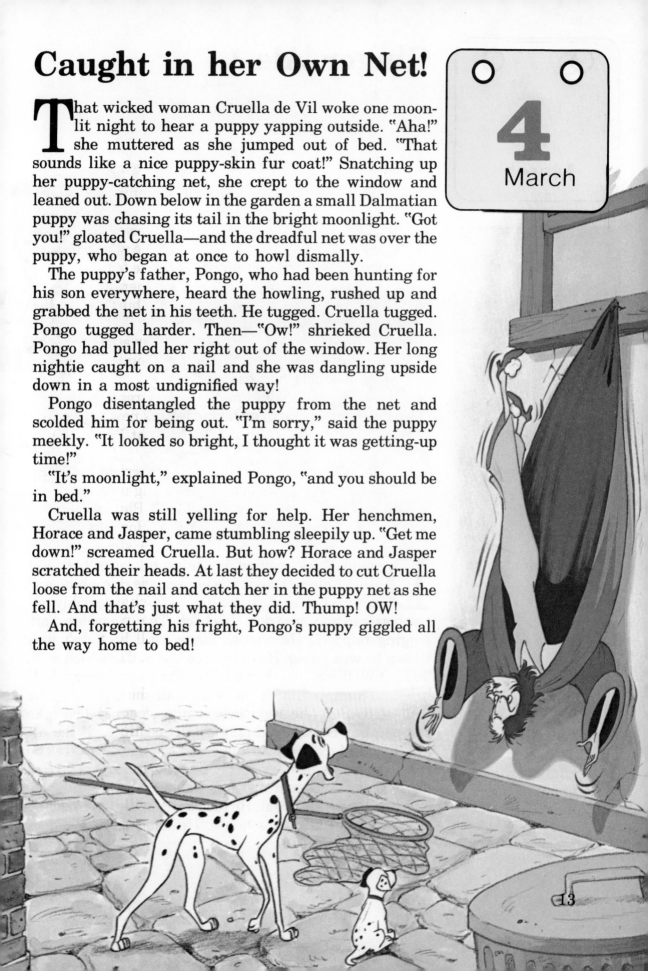

That wicked woman Cruella de Vil woke one moonlit night to hear a puppy yapping outside. "Aha!" she muttered as she jumped out of bed. "That sounds like a nice puppy-skin fur coat!" Snatching up her puppy-catching net, she crept to the window and leaned out. Down below in the garden a small Dalmatian puppy was chasing its tail in the bright moonlight. "Got you!" gloated Cruella—and the dreadful net was over the puppy, who began at once to howl dismally.

The puppy's father, Pongo, who had been hunting for his son everywhere, heard the howling, rushed up and grabbed the net in his teeth. He tugged. Cruella tugged. Pongo tugged harder. Then—"Ow!" shrieked Cruella. Pongo had pulled her right out of the window. Her long nightie caught on a nail and she was dangling upside down in a most undignified way!

Pongo disentangled the puppy from the net and scolded him for being out. "I'm sorry," said the puppy meekly. "It looked so bright, I thought it was getting-up time!"

"It's moonlight," explained Pongo, "and you should be in bed."

Cruella was still yelling for help. Her henchmen, Horace and Jasper, came stumbling sleepily up. "Get me down!" screamed Cruella. But how? Horace and Jasper scratched their heads. At last they decided to cut Cruella loose from the nail and catch her in the puppy net as she fell. And that's just what they did. Thump! OW!

And, forgetting his fright, Pongo's puppy giggled all the way home to bed!

13

Ginger Ale

Bambi: "What animal gets along with the least amount of food?"
Thumper: "The moth. It eats nothing but holes."

Donald Duck was on his bike, taking a bottle of ginger ale to Daisy. It's not easy to ride a bike and carry a bottle of ginger ale, so Donald sensibly put the bottle in a knapsack on his back. Then he pedaled off, singing happily. He was so happy that he didn't look where he was going. He didn't see the notice which said, 'ROAD WORKS', so—bump! The bike leaped over a half brick. Thump! His front wheel dived into a hole. And—CRASH!—he rode into a pile of sand! The bike stopped but Donald didn't. He hurtled through the air and landed face down in some wet cement. SPLOT! The road workers were very cross about the mess Donald had made of their cement, so he got on his bike and rode away as fast as he could. He took more care this time and soon arrived at Daisy's house. He knocked at the door and Daisy opened it.

"HELP!" she screamed. "Go away!"

"But it's me," said Donald.

"No, it's not!" shrieked Daisy. "You're a ghost! You're all gray and shiny and wet and—ugh!"

"It's only cement," said Donald. "I've brought you a present—here!" He gave Daisy the ginger ale. But it had been so shaken up that when she opened it, ginger ale fizzed out in a fountain! Daisy gave a loud shriek, shut her eyes and held the bottle as far away from her as she could. It sprayed all over Donald, who yelled almost as loudly as Daisy! The ginger ale washed most of the cement off, though, and Daisy suddenly began to laugh. "Oh, Donald," she gasped, "you *do* look funny!"

"I don't *feel* funny," grumbled Donald. "I feel sticky!"

"You'd better come in and wash the rest of that stuff off," said Daisy. "And thank you for the ginger ale. It was a very kind thought!"

When Donald was nice and clean, Daisy mixed the ginger ale that was left with some ice-cold lemonade, and they drank it on the lawn.

"All's well that ends well!" sighed Donald happily.

15

An Apron for Grumpy

In the seven dwarfs' house, Grumpy was making a cake. "Nobody else makes cakes as nice as mine," he grumbled, "so I'd better do it myself."

"You should a-tchoo!—wear an apron," snuffled Sneezy.

"I've got an apron!" beamed Happy. "Here it is!"

"I *hate* aprons," snapped Grumpy. "And that one's all darns and patches."

"It'll keep you clean," said Doc sensibly.

So Grumpy put on the apron, but he was so cross about it that all the other dwarfs except Sleepy went out to do some gardening. Sleepy, of course, was asleep.

Grumpy glared at Sleepy, and glared at his apron. Then he had an idea. He took off the apron and woke Sleepy.

"Hey!" he shouted. "Time you did some work, Sleepy. I'm busy making a cake and the others are out gardening. You can do some ironing!"

"All right," yawned Sleepy. He stumbled sleepily over to the ironing board and started to iron Grumpy's apron. To and fro he went with the hot iron . . . and then he dozed off where he stood, leaning on the iron which lay in the middle of Grumpy's apron.

Walrus: "What is covered in feathers and has a twenty-five-foot wingspan?"
Carpenter: "A five-ton parakeet?"

Grumpy went on mixing his cake. A smell of burning came from the ironing board, but Grumpy took no notice. He tipped his mixture into a cake pan and put it in the oven.

Just then the door opened and Snow White came in. "Sleepy," she cried, "wake up! That's dreadfully dangerous!"

"Eh? What?" Sleepy opened his eyes and gasped with horror when he saw the big black burn mark on Grumpy's apron.

"Grumpy," scolded Snow White, "why did you let Sleepy do that? You must have smelled burning!"

"I was making a cake," sulked Grumpy.

Snow White laughed. "So you were!" she said. "Just look at your jacket, covered with flour! What you need is an apron!" She got out a new, pink, flowered apron and tied it on Grumpy. "There," she smiled, "you *do* look nice!"

"You *do!*" chorused the dwarfs, coming in from the garden.

"You *do!*" yawned Sleepy.

"I *do?*" asked Grumpy. "Well, well!" And for once, he smiled, too!

17

The Solid Silver Salad Bowl

Mickey Mouse had just put his trash can out for the trash man to empty when he saw Uncle Scrooge coming along the road. As he passed each can, the mean old duck lifted its lid and peered in.

"Looking for something, Uncle Scrooge?" called Mickey.

"Trash cans are always worth looking in," said Uncle Scrooge. "Somebody might have thrown something valuable away."

Mickey laughed. "I see! You'd better have a good look in my can, then—I've just thrown out the solid silver salad bowl. Fed up with cleaning it—got a plastic one instead!" And Mickey went indoors, grinning. He didn't own *any* kind of salad bowl, let alone a solid silver one! Looking through the window, he saw Uncle Scrooge take the lid off the trash can.

"Solid silver salad bowl," muttered the old miser. "Probably a joke. Mickey is just stupid enough, though . . . he *might* have thrown it out." He began to fish about in the rubbish. Paper bags, fish bones, empty cans—and

then Uncle Scrooge saw a glint of something bright at the bottom of the can. The solid silver salad bowl! It must be! Things came flying out of the can as Uncle Scrooge dug his way downwards. The shining thing was right at the bottom, just out of his reach. He leaned in as far as he could, and reached a little further, then—CLANG! He fell in head first and was wedged there upside down, his short legs kicking wildly!

Mickey rushed out of the house just as the trash men arrived. "Are you throwing this person away, sir?" one of them asked Mickey.

"Don't tempt me!" said Mickey. He and the trash men hauled out Uncle Scrooge, who was covered with rubbish.

"Never mind!" cackled the old miser. "Look at my solid silver salad bowl!" He held out—an empty sardine can! His spectacles were covered with rubbish and he couldn't see a thing. When Mickey wiped them for him and he saw what he had got he was furious!

"I'm going home," he snapped.

"Don't forget your solid silver salad bowl!" grinned Mickey. And he and the trash men laughed so much that they had to lean against the trash cart for support!

Noises at Night

Mowgli was dozing under a tree one morning when his friend Bagheera came loping through the jungle. "Hello, little one," he said, when he saw Mowgli. "Are you still sleeping at this hour of the morning? It's time for all animals to be up and busy."

Mowgli yawned and rubbed his eyes. "It's all very well," he grumbled, "but those monkeys kept me awake half the night. They've come to live in the trees near me and they're always having parties—at least, that's what it sounds like."

"Why?" inquired Bagheera. "What do they do?"

"They scream and chatter and scratch and throw nuts," said Mowgli, "as well as rush up and down the branches and knock half the leaves off. It's *awful!*"

"I'll have a word with them," promised Bagheera. But the monkeys were all snoozing high in the treetops, looking even more tired than Mowgli, and when Bagheera suggested they should sleep at night instead of in the day, they made a lot of rude remarks, pelted him with bananas and went to sleep again. Bagheera went away and thought hard.

20

That evening, as the sun was setting, the monkeys woke up for their nightly revels. Mowgli, snuggled in his cave with his fingers in his ears to try and stop the noise, was startled to find a black, furry creature beside him. It was Bagheera. "Are you asleep, little one?" he whispered.

"No," said Mowgli gloomily. "How could I be with all that rumpus outside?"

"Good!" grinned Bagheera. "I'm about to make a lot *more* noise and I wouldn't like to wake you."

Then he went to the cave's entrance, pointed his black nose at the sky and howled a long, high-pitched, quavering yell. There was instant silence from the monkeys. Mowgli grinned. "What an awful noise, Bagheera!" he said.

"It is, isn't it!" agreed Bagheera smugly. "I don't often get the chance of a good howling practice. Have the monkeys gone?"

Mowgli peeped out. "Yes!" he grinned. "Every single one!" Then he snuggled down beside his warm, purring friend, and they both slept peacefully all night long!

Hooked Up!

Peter Pan had made an enormous kite. He had great fun zooming through the clouds with it.

"Lunchtime, Peter!" called Wendy. Peter dived down and looped the kite string round a tree to stop it sailing off again.

Peter and Wendy had just finished lunch when they heard heavy footsteps. "Shiver me timbers!" boomed a voice. "A kite! A *big* kite!" Peter and Wendy rushed out to find Captain Hook undoing the kite string from the tree.

"That's *Peter's* kite!" cried Wendy indignantly.

"'Tis mine now, me hearties," grinned Captain Hook.

Peter nudged Wendy and whispered, "It's too big for him."

"Too big?" roared Hook, overhearing. "Rubbish!"

A sudden gust of wind swept the kite up into the sky and Hook soared up with it. "Aa-aagh!" he roared. "Put me down!"

Peter and Wendy laughed and laughed. Captain Hook and the kite drifted right out across the lagoon. "If we rescue you," shouted Peter, "can we have our kite back?"

"No!" bellowed Hook. "*I* want it!"

At that moment the wind dropped. Hook and the kite fell—splash!—into the water where the crocodile was waiting. Mouth open, it swam towards Hook, who was tangled up in the kite.

"Oh, Peter!" cried kindhearted Wendy. "Quickly!"

They flew out to Captain Hook, snatched him out of the water and dumped him on a small island.

"Th—thank you," shivered Hook, dripping.

Peter and Wendy laughed as they flew away with their kite, but Hook didn't laugh. And neither did the crocodile!

Breakfast in Bed!

One cold morning Donald Duck decided to have breakfast in bed. He would have porridge and boiled eggs and toast and lots of cups of tea. But if he wanted breakfast in bed he would have to get up and cook it.

"Brr! Bed's the warmest place, Pluto!" he shivered. Pluto looked hopeful. "You want breakfast too, do you?" said Donald. "Right. Yours is in the freezer." He got out a slab of frozen dog meat and dropped it with a clang on Pluto's plate, then started cooking porridge.

Pluto licked at his breakfast. It was so cold that his tongue almost stuck to it. "Yes, bed's the warmest place," chortled Donald happily as he put his eggs in the skillet. "Nothing like breakfast in bed. Hey! Take your meat out of the toaster!"

Pluto dropped his meat back on the plate with another clang and explained that he was only trying to thaw it out. But Donald wasn't listening. "Beautifully warm in bed," he prattled, "with lots of tea and the morning paper. Warm as toast!"

Pluto quietly picked up his dog meat and sneaked out. Donald arranged his breakfast very nicely on a tray, with egg-cozies on his eggs and a tea-cozy on his teapot, and carried it into his bedroom.

"This is going to be *lovely*!" he beamed, getting into bed. Then—"OW! EEK! YOWP!! What's this awful cold thing in my bed?"

"It's my breakfast," beamed Pluto, "thawing out. You did say bed's the warmest place!"

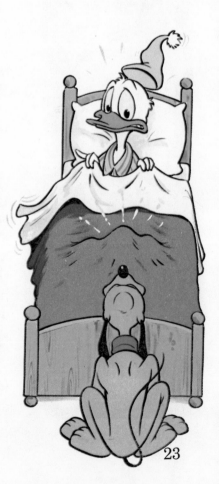

23

The Yak Thief

Bernard and Bianca, the two brave little mice from the International Rescue Aid Society, knew that Madame Medusa was planning to capture little Penny again. She and her assistant, Snoops, had once kidnapped the little orphaned girl to find a priceless diamond. They smuggled themselves into the Pawn Shop Boutique and stared around.

"The typewriter!" breathed Bianca. "She uses it for notes to her henchmen. Let's change the letters around —it'll delay her for a bit while she puts it right."

Bernard got out his little screwdriver and started to change over the letters. He changed the G for the Y, the U for the A and the N for the K—and then a key scratched in the lock. "Quick! Hide!" gasped Bianca. From behind the telephone directories they saw Madame Medusa come in. She snatched up the telephone, dialed, then hissed, "Snoops? Listen. We need the girl again. I have a plan . . . No, stupid, not over the telephone, you don't know who's listening. I'll leave a message on the typewriter. OK? And—BRING WHAT I ASK. It's *vital.* Good-bye."

She slammed down the receiver, rattled off a few words on the typewriter and rushed out, slamming the door.

Huey: "Three men fell into the water, but only two got their hair wet."
Dewey: "Why?"
Huey: "One of them was bald."

"Look!" whispered Bianca. "She's written, 'Come to school 3.30 with yak'. A *yak*?"

"Those are the letters I changed!" giggled Bernard. "It should be GUN, not YAK! What a good thing she's an expert typist—she doesn't have to look at what she's typing."

Heavy footsteps sounded outside, and the mice hid again as Snoops came in. He read the note and scratched his head. "A *yak*?" he said. "But that's a darn great shaggy cow. I'll have to steal one from the Zoo. Must be mad, wanting a yak." Grumbling, he went out.

The mice were in fits of giggles. "I wonder if Orville the Albatross is about?" said Bianca. She looked out of the window—and luckily Orville was circling the house. He gave them a lift to the Zoo, where they had a bird's-eye view of Snoops being arrested for attempted yak-stealing.

"I hope Madame Medusa hasn't managed to kidnap Penny in spite of not having a gun," said Bianca.

"Don't worry!" grinned Bernard. "When the police see that note, she'll be arrested as an accomplice yak-thief!"

25

Sum Honey!

One day Kanga and Roo went to see Pooh Bear. "Pooh," said Kanga, "it's time Roo went to school." Pooh looked puzzled. "I am a bear of very little brain," he said, "so I don't know about schools. Let's go and ask Wol."

They found Wol at home in his oak tree, blinking rather crossly. When he heard what they wanted he almost smiled. "I can teach little Roo everything," he said. "We will start with sums."

"What's sums?" asked Roo.

"Sums are adding up," said Wol. "Or taking away. If you have one bee and another bee what have you got?"

"One buzz," said Pooh.

"No, Pooh," said Wol patiently. "You have two bees."

"*And* one buzz!" said Roo.

Wol sighed. "Let's try again," he said. "Add two carrots and two carrots."

"You'd have one Rabbit," said Kanga. "You know what Rabbit is like."

"Oh dear," muttered Wol. "We'd better try taking away. Now, Kanga and Roo are two animals, right? Take Roo from Kanga and you have——"

"A black eye," said Kanga promptly.

"Oh, all right," Wol soothed her, "let's try something

else. Suppose you have three apples. Take two away, what's left?"

"Not enough," said Pooh. Roo nodded intelligently. "That's right," he agreed.

Wol groaned and shut his eyes.

"Perhaps you could show us how proper counting is done," suggested Pooh. "Then we'd get on better."

"Certainly," said Wol. "I'll count the apples on this tree. One, two, three, four, fix, seleven, bine, sen. There."

"Is that all of them?" asked Kanga.

"There are more," said Wol, "but I don't want to bore you."

"When I count my honey pots," said Pooh, "it's not quite like that. I thought there were thirteen pots of honey on my shelf this morning and when I ate one there were twelve. But I may be wrong."

"Yes, Pooh," said Wol kindly, "you are. But never mind."

"I won't," said Pooh. So he and Kanga and Roo went back to Pooh's house to eat pot of honey number twelve.

"I like your sort of sums, Pooh," said Roo stickily. "This is a *nice* school!"

The Painters

Shere Khan: "Why did Mowgli look over the wall?"
Baloo: "UM, err, ummm!"
Shere Khan: "Because he couldn't see through it!"

Daisy Duck's nieces, April, May and June, were very naughty one day. They found Auntie Daisy's make-up bag open on the dressing table and picked up her stick of mascara.

"I know how Auntie Daisy does her eyelashes," said April.

"And eye shadow," said May.

"Like this!" said June.

And in no time those naughty girls were busy painting their eyelashes black and their eyelids blue and their cheeks pink. They stuck on curly false eyelashes and found lots of lipstick in different shades of pink, and tried on all Daisy's wigs. They had a lovely time, but they used far too much of everything and they looked *frightful!*

Suddenly they heard the front door bang. "Auntie Daisy's come home!" they gasped. "Oh, dear!"

Daisy Duck went straight upstairs to take off her hat, and caught her nieces red-handed—or, rather, red-faced!

"You naughty girls!" she scolded—but she had to laugh at their rainbow-colored faces!

"Go and scrub it off," she told them. They found the make-up very hard to get off, and when they came back, pink and shining, Daisy said, "If you like painting, I've got the very job for you. The spare room needs decorating. You'll find paint and brushes in there. Off you go!"

April, May and June found the big paint brushes very heavy, but at last they finished the room.

"Whew!" gasped April.

"Done at last," sighed May.

But June giggled. "At least," she pointed out, "we won't have to scrub *this* paint off!"

Wolf at the Fair

Clarabelle Cow:
"I'd like some pork, and make it lean, please."
Stromboli: "Certainly, madam. Which way?"

The three little pigs were on their way to the fair, sitting in the back of a neighboring farmer's cart.

"Nice to have a lift," said Fifer Pig. "Look—is that another passenger?"

A figure in long skirts and a sun bonnet was waving an oddly gray thumb by the roadside. "It's the Big Bad Wolf!" gasped Practical Pig. "I do hope the farmer doesn't stop!"

The farmer didn't stop. But the Big Bad Wolf got to the fair somehow, and once there he took off his disguise and set about catching himself a roast pork dinner! The three little pigs kept seeing his grinning face everywhere they went. At a game stand he was wearing dark glasses and pretending to be the proprietor. On the merry-go-round he was crouched on all fours beside the painted horses, hoping that the little pigs would jump on *his* back by mistake.

"I wish he'd join that line of wooden ducks," said Fifer

Pig, fingering a rifle thoughtfully at the shooting gallery.

"He's not that silly," said Fiddler Pig gloomily. "I think we ought to go home. It's no fun with him here."

"He'll make a mistake sooner or later," said Practical Pig. "You'll see. Now, let's all have an ice cream and cheer up."

Licking their ice creams, the little pigs wandered into a tent labeled 'Dog Show'. There were all sorts of dogs there—little fluffy dogs, big curly dogs and a huge, gray dog. "*That's* not a dog!" squealed Fifer. "It's the Big Bad Wolf!" agreed Fiddler.

Practical Pig finished his ice cream, thinking hard. Then he found a big board and a thick black marker, and wrote, 'ALL DOGS TO BE ON A LEASH'. He propped his notice up, and waited. Soon people started to complain. "That big gray dog should be on a leash. He looks dangerous," they said. An official tied the Big Bad Wolf up firmly, and the little pigs slipped happily out of the tent.

"What a good idea!" giggled Fifer and Fiddler. "The other dogs have owners who will untie them, but the Wolf will be tied up all day!"

They had a lovely time at the fair—and the sound of howling from the Dog-Show tent didn't spoil it at all!

31

The Picnic Dragon

Bambi's friend Thumper had been telling him a story about a fierce dragon that blew flames from its mouth and chased people. Bambi was rather frightened, but Thumper said, "Don't be silly! There are no *real* dragons—it's only a story!" So Bambi felt better and went scampering off to find something to play with.

He came to a grassy clearing—and stopped in astonishment. There were people sitting there, with a cloth spread on the ground and all sorts of things to eat, and—right in the middle of the cloth was a thing which spat a ring of blue flame. "A dragon!" thought Bambi. It was rather smaller than Thumper had said and it had no scales, but even so . . .

Bambi thought of running away, but the dragon showed no signs of coming towards him, so he thought it might be safe to stay. One of the people put a round metal thing on top of the dragon. The metal thing had a lid on top and a handle to pick it up by and a spout at one side, and after a while, to Bambi's terror, steam began to hiss out of the spout. He rushed away through the forest until he found his mother and cuddled up to her, shaking with fright. "A dragon!" he gasped. "And another dragon on top! Flames and steam!"

Bambi's mother explained about picnic stoves and kettles, and Bambi *was* glad to hear that they didn't chase people through forests! After that, he kept well away from picnickers, though,—just in case!

Piano on Skates

The seven dwarfs were all very excited because it was Dopey's birthday and they were going to have a party. Snow White was busy making cakes and all the dwarfs except Dopey were getting everything ready. Dopey was scooting about on his new birthday roller skates.

"Let's move the piano into the big room," suggested Happy. "Then we can play Musical Chairs!"

"Oh, *yes*!" agreed the others. "Come on!"

The piano lived in a small room just right for practicing scales. The dwarfs rushed in and started to push the piano out. "Phew! It's heavy!" groaned Sleepy.

It *was* heavy. The dwarfs managed to push it as far as the door but they couldn't get it any further. "Where's Dopey?" growled Grumpy. "It's *his* birthday—he should help!" Dopey zoomed up on his roller skates. "Of course I'll help!" he beamed. But every time he pushed, his roller-skated feet shot out from under him and he fell flat on his face.

"What you should do," said Doc, "is to put the roller skates on the piano. Then instead of *you* slipping, *it* would!"

"What a good idea!" chuckled the others. "Come on, Dopey!"

Dopey didn't really want to take his new skates off, but at last he did and they fitted them under the piano. Then—whee! The piano slid into the big room as easily as anything.

"Oh, Dopey," smiled Snow White, "how *clever* of you!"

And because it was Dopey's birthday, nobody told Snow White that it was really Doc's idea!

33

Women Drivers!

Bashful: "Your cough sounds much better this morning."
Grumpy: "It should—I've been practicing all night."

D onald Duck's nephews Huey, Dewey and Louie made themselves a go-cart. The front pair of wheels could be moved from side to side so the go-cart could turn corners, and it was great fun.

Daisy Duck's nieces April, May and June wanted to play with the go-cart, too, but Huey said, "*We* built it!" "It's *ours*!" agreed Dewey. "Not for *girls*!" scoffed Louie.

The girls had a good idea. Tucked away in the garage was the big old baby buggy they had ridden in as babies. "*Just* as good as a go-cart," said April. "Bigger!" smiled May. "More comfy!" laughed June. So they pushed the buggy to the hilltop and all scrambled in. "Off we go!" they shouted. "Whee!"

The buggy soon gathered speed, bumping and jumping over the grass. April, May and June had to hold on tight to avoid being thrown out! As they neared the bottom they wondered how to stop. Unlike the boys' go-cart, the buggy had no steering. It hurtled on—and right in their path was the go-cart!

"Look out!" shouted April, May and June. But—too late! The buggy crashed into the go-cart and the body of the buggy broke away from its wheels and somersaulted across the grass, spilling the girls out as it went.

"Women drivers!" sniffed Huey. But Dewey said, "That buggy can't be steered. They couldn't help it." And Louie offered, "Let's rebuild their buggy as a proper go-cart!" "Thank you!" beamed the girls.

And with two go-carts they had splendid races all afternoon.

Nest Rescue

Uncle Scrooge:
"Do you have any dogs going cheap?"
Clarabelle Cow:
"Sorry, sir. All our dogs go 'Bowwow'!"

Dumbo was out with his friend Timothy Mouse when he saw smoke coming out of a cottage window. "Goodness me!" he cried. "It must be on fire!"

He rushed to the window and saw an old lady kneeling by the fire. Smoke was billowing out of the chimney. "Drat it!" muttered the old lady. "Why won't this fire burn? My sticks are nice and dry but there's no draft."

Timothy Mouse hopped in through the window, scuttled across the floor and stared up the chimney. There was no daylight to be seen at the top—and a piece of twig fell down and hit him on the nose!

Timothy scuttled back to his friend, Dumbo. "I think there's something on the chimney," he said, rubbing his nose. "Something twiggy."

"Twiggy . . ." mused Dumbo. "Aha!" With Timothy on

his back, he flew up to the rooftop and found a large, untidy nest piled on top of the chimney, with a bird sitting on it.

"Help!" squawked the bird, scared at the sight of Dumbo.

"You *do* need help," said Dumbo. "Your nest has a fire under it!"

"What?" shrieked the bird. "Oh, no! My eggs will be fried!"

"Slide your nest on to my back," said Dumbo. "Timothy will help you. Then we'll carry your eggs to a safe place."

The mother bird flew beside Dumbo, and they put the nest in a hollow tree where she settled down gratefully.

The old lady was grateful too, because with the nest gone, her fire burned beautifully!

Pluto's Pajamas

"Pluto," said Minnie Mouse one day, "what a *scruffy* dog you are!"

Pluto gazed up, surprised.

"Just look at that dog over there," went on Minnie, "that golden retriever. He's a nice yellow color all over, and his coat shines as if he'd just washed it. Beautiful!"

Pluto didn't wait to hear any more. He slunk home and stared at himself in the mirror. He looked the same as usual, he thought—but perhaps Minnie liked yellow dogs better. Pluto had an idea. He put on Minnie's yellow silk pajamas, then looked again at his reflection. Much

Horace: "I say, waiter, what's this fly doing in my soup?"
Tony: "The breast stroke I think, sir!"

38

better! But what else had Minnie said? 'His coat shines as if he'd just washed it.' Right! Still wearing Minnie's pajamas, he turned on the tap and washed himself—and the pajamas—all over!

When Minnie came home, Pluto bounced up to her, feeling sure she would be pleased to see him so yellow and shining. But she wasn't!

"Pluto!" she shouted. "What *are* you doing in my pajamas? And why are they dripping wet? You *silly* dog!"

Pluto's ears drooped. First he was scruffy and now he was silly! He decided that it was more comfortable to be scruffy and dry than silly and wet, so he peeled off Minnie's pajamas and jumped about in the sunshine until he was dry again.

When Minnie saw him she smiled. "That's better!" she said. "Even if you are a bit scruffy, it's nice to have you looking like Pluto again!"

And Pluto felt very happy.

Grumpy's Busy Day

"Lucky Snow White!" grumbled Grumpy, the dwarf. "You have to stay at home in the house all day, doing nothing! If you worked in the mine with Dopey, Happy, Doc, Sneezy, Sleepy, Bashful and me, you'd KNOW what work is!"

Grumpy looked cross, but Snow White smiled.

"Well, Grumpy," she said, "today I'm not going to stay in the house 'doing nothing', as you say. I'm going to buy myself a new dress and shoes. I'll be at the shops all day, so you, Grumpy, can stay at home and do my spring cleaning for me. I will leave you a list of the things that have to be done."

"A day at home, doing hardly anything!" chuckled Grumpy. "I'll like that better than going to the mine with the others and working hard."

Dopey, Happy, Doc, Sneezy, Sleepy and Bashful set off for the mine. Grumpy waved good-bye to them at the door, and he waved to Snow White as she set off to catch the bus to town. Then he went indoors to look at the list Snow White had left him.

JOB 1. MAKE THE BEDS, said the list.

"That's soon done," sniffed Grumpy.

But there were seven little beds to make, as well as Snow White's bigger bed. Grumpy wasn't expert at making beds, and it took him a long time to finish them. By then he was so tired and thirsty that he sat down and had a drink of orange juice and looked at the list again.

JOB 2. WASH UP THE BREAKFAST THINGS.

"That will only take two minutes," thought Grumpy.

Now, there was a lot of washing-up—seven little cups, saucers, bowls, plates and spoons. Snow White's bigger cup, saucer, bowl, plate and spoon had to be washed, too, as well as the teapot and frying pan. Then they had to be dried and put away in the cupboard. After all that, Grumpy was so tired and hungry that he had a biscuit to eat while he looked at the list again.

JOB 3. WASH TOMORROW'S SHIRTS AND SOCKS.

"Shouldn't take long," said Grumpy.

Grumpy fetched Dopey's, Happy's, Doc's, Sneezy's, Bashful's and Sleepy's shirts, as well as his own. They all needed a very good wash because they had been worn in

Jasper: "Hey, waiter, there's a bug on my lettuce!"

Tony: "Hush please, sir, otherwise they'll all want one!"

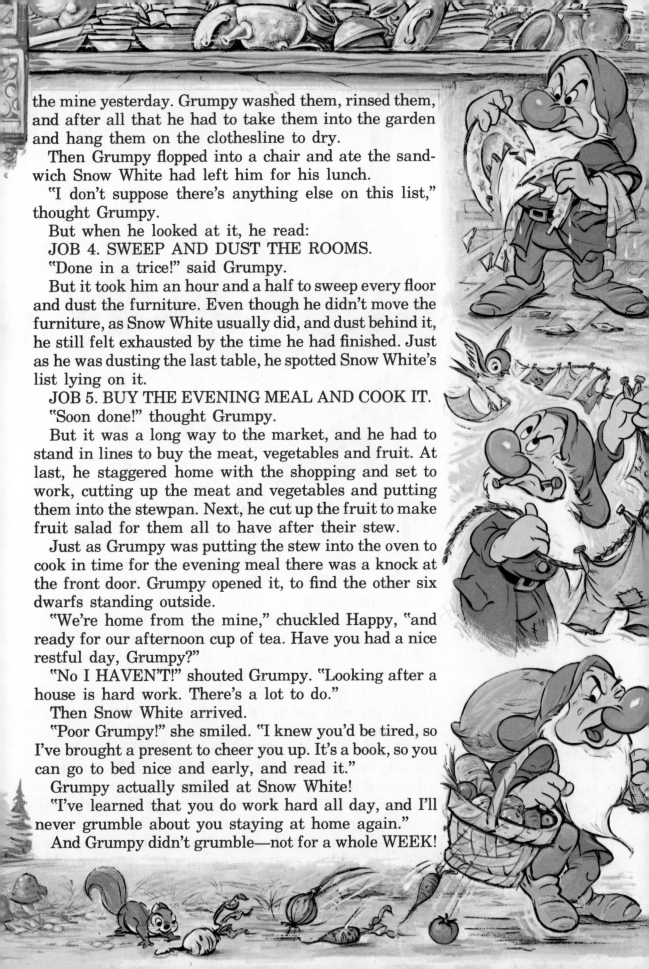

the mine yesterday. Grumpy washed them, rinsed them, and after all that he had to take them into the garden and hang them on the clothesline to dry.

Then Grumpy flopped into a chair and ate the sandwich Snow White had left him for his lunch.

"I don't suppose there's anything else on this list," thought Grumpy.

But when he looked at it, he read:

JOB 4. SWEEP AND DUST THE ROOMS.

"Done in a trice!" said Grumpy.

But it took him an hour and a half to sweep every floor and dust the furniture. Even though he didn't move the furniture, as Snow White usually did, and dust behind it, he still felt exhausted by the time he had finished. Just as he was dusting the last table, he spotted Snow White's list lying on it.

JOB 5. BUY THE EVENING MEAL AND COOK IT.

"Soon done!" thought Grumpy.

But it was a long way to the market, and he had to stand in lines to buy the meat, vegetables and fruit. At last, he staggered home with the shopping and set to work, cutting up the meat and vegetables and putting them into the stewpan. Next, he cut up the fruit to make fruit salad for them all to have after their stew.

Just as Grumpy was putting the stew into the oven to cook in time for the evening meal there was a knock at the front door. Grumpy opened it, to find the other six dwarfs standing outside.

"We're home from the mine," chuckled Happy, "and ready for our afternoon cup of tea. Have you had a nice restful day, Grumpy?"

"No I HAVEN'T!" shouted Grumpy. "Looking after a house is hard work. There's a lot to do."

Then Snow White arrived.

"Poor Grumpy!" she smiled. "I knew you'd be tired, so I've brought a present to cheer you up. It's a book, so you can go to bed nice and early, and read it."

Grumpy actually smiled at Snow White!

"I've learned that you do work hard all day, and I'll never grumble about you staying at home again."

And Grumpy didn't grumble—not for a whole WEEK!

The Modest Hero

Thomas O'Malley was prowling hungrily down the street one morning when he saw a bottle of milk standing on a doorstep. He licked his lips. A saucer of nice, creamy milk was just what he fancied. The trouble was, though, that milk was very difficult to get out of the bottle—that is, if you happened to be a cat with rather large paws.

Suddenly a little bird flew down and perched on the top of the bottle. With a couple of sharp pecks, it made a hole in the top and then took a big sip of cream. Thomas was furious. It was bad enough that he couldn't get into the bottle himself, and much worse to see a cheeky little bird stealing it!

Thomas's tail twitched. If he couldn't have milk, then a tasty breakfast of bird would do very nicely instead. He flattened himself on the pavement and crept very slowly towards the bird, which was too intent on stealing milk to take any notice. Closer and closer Thomas crept and then—pounce!—he leaped at the bird, but, with a

squawk of alarm, the little bird flew up just in time. The milk bottle rocked dangerously and Thomas put his paw on the top to steady it. If the bottle broke, he'd *never* get any milk!

Then he noticed that the door was open and a little old lady was standing there. "What a kind pussycat you are!" she beamed. "I've had *such* trouble with the naughty birds stealing my milk and it's *sweet* of you to chase them away, *and* to steady the bottle in case it broke!"

Thomas felt rather ashamed of himself, but he tried his best to look like a modest hero. "Come along in!" invited the old lady. "The least I can do is give you some milk!"

So Thomas sat by the fire and drank his milk, and ate all the rind from the old lady's breakfast bacon. It was really more than he deserved, he thought, but then he looked at the old lady's smiling face and felt quite pleased with himself—as usual!

43

Custard and Mustard

"**D**inner!" shouted Practical Pig. "Fifer! Fiddler! Time for dinner!" But there was no answer from his two naughty brothers. "It's too bad," muttered Practical Pig. "They've been late for dinner every day this week. I'll have to teach them a lesson." But how? Practical Pig thought hard as he put the apple pie back in the oven to keep warm. Then his eye fell on the jug of custard standing on the table.

Practical Pig chuckled as he put the custard safely in the cupboard. He made a jug of very strong *mustard* and left it in the middle of the table. Then he went upstairs for a nap.

Heavy footsteps approaching the house woke Practical Pig. Fifer and Fiddler, home at last! He peeped through a crack in the floorboards to see if his trick would work. Heavens! It wasn't Fifer and Fiddler! It was the Big Bad Wolf!

"Now," growled the Big Bad Wolf, "what is there to eat in this house? What's in this jug? M'm, *custard!*" He seized the jug of mustard and poured it into his mouth . . .

"Aa—aa—rgh!" he howled—and rushed out of the house back into the forest, almost knocking over Fifer and Fiddler who had just come in from playing.

Practical Pig came downstairs to find his brothers shivering with fright, but they were soon laughing when they heard about the Big Bad Wolf and the mustard. Then they sat down to apple pie with custard, not mustard, and promised they'd never be late again.

Cream Puffs and a Scarecrow

"Unca Donald," shouted Donald Duck's three nephews, rushing in, "there are birds in your garden, eating all the peas!"

Donald was tying his bow tie. "Daisy is coming to lunch," he beamed. Then he looked stern. "So just you keep out of the way. No tricks!"

"No, Unca Donald," promised the ducklings, trooping out again. The greedy birds were still there.

"Let's make a scarecrow!" suggested Huey.

"A *big* scarecrow," agreed Dewey.

"Just like Unca Donald," chimed in Louie.

They stuffed a sack with straw and stuck feathers all over it, used coal for eyes and a carrot for a beak.

"Clothes?" wondered Huey.

"Not Unca Donald's," said Dewey.

"He said keep out of the way," nodded Louie.

But their mother gave them an old dress and a hair ribbon and soon they had made a splendid *lady* scarecrow.

"She's pretty!" smiled Huey.

"Here's Unca Donald!" warned Dewey.

"Out of the way!" urged Louie.

The ducklings hid as Donald strutted out. He saw the scarecrow and gasped. "Daisy!" he beamed. "You're early!" He rushed up to the scarecrow and hugged it—and at that moment the real Daisy Duck arrived.

"I've brought you some cream puffs," she began. Then—"Donald! You beast! Hugging another girl! Oh!"

"Eh?" gasped Donald. "I—" Daisy thrust the whole bag of cream puffs into his open beak and rushed away.

"Awk!" quacked Donald. He dropped the cream puffs and galloped after Daisy.

"Poor Unca Donald!" sighed Huey.

"Will he want the cream puffs?" wondered Dewey.

"I don't think so!" beamed Louie.

So they ate them. They were *lovely*!

The Easy Way

24
March

Dopey: "I woke up last night with the feeling that my watch was gone."
Happy: "And was it?"
Dopey: "No, but it was going."

It had not rained for a long time, and the March Hare's garden was very dry. "I shall have to water it," he said to himself. "Bother. I do hate carrying cans. But, no water—no carrots!" Then he thought, "If I fit a pump to the old well, I can water it the easy way!"

The March Hare rushed into his workshop. All morning, as the sun shone brighter and the carrots wilted, there were sounds of hammering and shouts of, "Bother it!" from the workshop. At midday the March Hare came out, hot and sticky and covered with grease. "Nearly done," he muttered. "All I need is one specially big screw. I wonder if the Dormouse has got one?"

He trotted off to the Dormouse's house and noticed that *his* carrots were looking beautifully green and fresh. "Different soil here," muttered the March Hare, banging on the door.

"Come in!" yawned a sleepy voice. The Dormouse was snoozing in an armchair.

"I need a large screw for my pump," said the March Hare. "I made it from an old vacuum cleaner and half a motorbike. I do things the easy way, you see, and water the garden with no effort. Oh, do wake *up*, Dormouse!"

"I do things the easy way, too," yawned the Dormouse, pointing a languid paw at the kitchen sink. A hose was attached to the cold tap and ran out through the window to the carrots. "Help yourself to screws," added the Dormouse, closing his eyes. "They're in the tool box."

The March Hare found a screw, rushed home and fitted it to his pump. He joined up the hoses, put one end in the well and the other on the carrots and switched on. There was a puff of smoke and a loud bang, and the pump fell to pieces! "*Drat!*" said the March Hare.

At that moment it began to rain. The March Hare grinned a sooty, oil-streaked grin. "There!" he said. "Silly old Dormouse has wasted all that water! I *knew* my way was easiest!"

The Secret Weapon

Tigger: "Did you know they're crossing sheep with kangaroos?"
Kanga: "Whatever for?"
Tigger: "To make woolly jumpers."

Bernard and Bianca, the little mice from the International Rescue Aid Society, were on their way home from a job, flying through the sky on the broad back of Orville the albatross.

"What black clouds!" said Bernard. "I hope we're not in for a storm."

"*I* hope we're not in for Madame Medusa," said Bianca. "She must be pretty cross by now at the way we keep outwitting her. She'll find a weapon against us one day."

"How awful," muttered Bernard nervously. The clouds thickened and soon there was a flash of lightning. Big drops of rain began to fall and it grew very dark. Orville peered through his goggles. "Can't see where I'm going," he said. Then suddenly—CRASH! Something had collided head on with Orville. "Help!" gasped Bernard. "It's Madame Medusa's new weapon!"

"Are you all right, Orville?" asked Bianca.

"Ergh!" gulped Orville. "There's a Thing on my goggles! Something leggy and wingy!"

"What is it?" squeaked the mice. For a moment there was panic aboard Orville—then a little voice was heard saying, "It's me—Evinrude!"

"Evinrude!" cried Bianca. "Thank goodness!" They helped the bedraggled little dragonfly safely on to Orville's back. "However did you get here?" asked Bernard.

"I was going home," said Evinrude, "and the storm was so fierce, I couldn't fly. And then I banged into you."

"We're so glad!" cried the little mice. "We thought you were Madame Medusa's secret weapon!"

"Oh, no," said Evinrude. "Just me!"

The storm cleared and Orville flew on homeward with his three happy passengers.

Heavy Boots

Morty: "I keep seeing little black spots before my eyes."
Ferdie: "Have you seen a doctor?"
Morty: "No, only little black spots."

"Dopey," smiled Snow White, "those boots are worn out. Would you like to come with me and buy some new ones?"

"I promised to help cement the new path," said Dopey, looking worried, "but I *do* need new boots."

"Leave it until tomorrow, then," said Snow White. "You mustn't break your promise."

Dopey scampered off to join the others, who were busy mixing cement. They had big bags of cement powder and a pile of sand and buckets of water, and Happy was stirring a huge heap of wet, sloppy cement. Doc was putting bits of wood along the sides of the new path to stop the cement spreading too far and the others were carrying bucketfuls of wet cement to pour in.

"Come on, Dopey," grumbled Grumpy. "Don't just stand there watching—carry a bucket like everyone else."

"I haven't got a bucket," said Dopey—but Grumpy had walked off and didn't hear him. Dopey stood and waited for one of the dwarfs to come back with an empty bucket, but they were all busy smoothing down the path and nobody came. After a bit, Dopey thought he would look for a bucket in the potting shed. He set out—and found that his boots were terribly heavy. He could hardly put one foot in front of the other!

Snow White came out to see how the path was getting on. "It's lovely!" she said. "And isn't it setting quickly —look, it's quite hard at this end!"

"My boots are quite hard, too," said poor Dopey. Snow White looked at his boots and laughed. "Oh, Dopey!" she said. "You've been standing in the cement! No wonder your boots are hard! You'd better take them off."

Dopey took his boots off, THUMP, THUMP, like two great, heavy rocks. "They're very heavy," he said.

"*Very* heavy!" agreed Snow White. "But never mind —I'll put them in the rock garden—they'll look lovely with flowers growing in them. And now I think we'd better buy you some new boots after all, don't you?"

"Yes," said Dopey, beaming. "I do!"

Burglars!

One dark night Thomas O'Malley was skulking around the back door of the house where the beautiful white cat, Duchess, lived. He hoped he might take her for an evening walk, but so far there was no sign of her.

Suddenly, Thomas was startled by a quiet footstep. He glanced around and saw a strange man creeping towards the house. He wore a black mask and dirty sneakers, and carried a large sack. Thomas blinked in amazement. He was even more amazed when the man began to climb up the drainpipe on the side of the house. "Why ever doesn't he use the door?" thought Thomas. "I would, if I was allowed in at all." But then Thomas noticed a bottle of milk on the doorstep which Edgar the butler had forgotten to take in. Thomas liked milk. Finally he had made a hole in the lid and was dipping his paw in the cream. He licked his paw and dipped again. Then again. Then—crash! The milk bottle fell off the step. Heavy footsteps pounded to the back door. "Ah!" shouted Edgar the butler. "Caught you!"

Panic-stricken, Thomas leaped for the windowsill. Edgar turned to cut off his escape—and saw the man in dirty sneakers with one foot over Madame Bonfamille's bedroom windowsill. "A burglar!" bellowed Edgar. "Stop, thief!"

From that moment there was pandemonium. The burglar disappeared into the house, the police were called and Thomas, taking advantage of the confusion, slipped into the kitchen for a long talk with Duchess, the beautiful white cat.

At last the burglar was caught and everything settled down again. Edgar found Thomas sitting by the fire with Duchess and said, "I don't hold with riffraff in this house, Thomas O'Malley—but I must admit, if it wasn't for you giving me the tip, we'd never have caught the burglar."

"My hero!" purred Duchess.

Thomas O'Malley smiled. Why spoil everything by admitting that he'd only been stealing the milk?

52

Primroses for Daisy

Daisy Duck's nieces, April, May and June, had been picking primroses. "We'll give them to Auntie Daisy," they said. "She likes flowers." But on the way home they met Uncle Scrooge. "What pretty flowers," he wheedled. "Nobody ever gives me flowers."

"Poor Uncle Scrooge," said April.

"What a shame," said May.

"Here you are," said June. And they gave Uncle Scrooge the whole bunch of primroses.

The old miser rushed home chuckling. He divided the big bunch of primroses into lots of little bunches and put them by his front gate with a notice, 'Primroses, 10¢ a bunch.' "Now I'll make lots of money," he chortled, as he went indoors.

April, May and June were very cross when they came past and saw the notice. "How mean!" they said. "Those primroses were a *present*!" And they crossed out '10¢ a bunch' on Uncle Scrooge's notice and wrote in big letters, 'FREE!' "There!" they giggled. "Serves him right!"

The next person to come past Uncle Scrooge's house was Donald Duck. "Primroses FREE!" he read. "Gosh! Uncle Scrooge must have turned over a new leaf!" He scooped up all the flowers and ran as fast as he could to Daisy's house, where April, May and June had just arrived. "A present!" he gasped. "From me!" And he gave Daisy Duck the primroses.

"Oh, *thank* you, Donald!" said Daisy. April, May and June were beaming. "Isn't that nice!" they said. "Auntie Daisy got the primroses after all!"

Donald didn't know what they meant, but he was too pleased to care!

53

Madam Mim and the Beanstalk

Scrooge McDuck gave his nephew Donald five tickets for the pantomime. Donald was astonished! Fancy mean Uncle Scrooge giving anything away!

On the way to the theatre, Donald and his nephews met the witch, Madam Mim, and asked her to join them. Madam Mim was thrilled!

But when they showed their tickets at the door the doorman pushed them outside. "These tickets are for LAST YEAR'S pantomime!" he cried.

"Huh!" snorted Donald. "Isn't that just like Uncle Scrooge!" Donald's nephews were upset! The posters for 'Jack and the Beanstalk' looked so exciting.

"You SHALL go to the pantomime," burbled Madam Mim. She waved her wand and WHOOSH! Donald's party found themselves inside the theatre, sitting in the very front row!

The pantomime had started, and Jack was watching the beanstalk grow. It was growing very JERKILY! "I'll climb it!" cried Jack bravely.

"Ooh!" gasped Madam Mim. "That beanstalk will never carry his weight!"

She took out her pocket-spellbook and flicked through the pages. "Izzy! Ozzy! Hear my talk! Grow and grow, you weedy beanstalk!"

Hey presto! The beanstalk grew and *grew* and GREW! It sprouted giant-sized green leaves, and, as it got thicker and thicker, poor Jack was lost in the greenery!

The beanstalk spread its tendrils right over the edge of the stage and into the orchestra pit! They wrapped themselves around the strings of the harp, and crawled right into the trumpets!

"Stop!" howled Donald, for now the tendrils of the beanstalk were creeping into the front row, and curling around Donald's sailor hat! "Take off the spell," he yelled to Madam Mim. "I can't!" she stammered! "I've lost the page that tells you how to do that!"

Donald and his party fled from the theatre, followed by all the other folk, and, outside, they watched the bean

tendrils pushing their way out of the windows! Soon the
theatre was covered in greenery!

"I must rush home and find my monster spellbook!"
quavered Madam Mim. "I MUST stop that beanstalk!"
And off she zoomed on her broomstick.

Donald and his nephews went home in a bad temper.
"Never mind! I've got your favorite supper," beamed
Daisy Duck. "Sausages and—fresh green beans!"

"BEANS! No!" they howled. "We never want to see a
bean again—NEVER!"

30 March

Clara the Clock!

Snow White: "Eat your artichoke."
Grumpy: "I arti-choke you for cooking this."

"Hallo, Donald!" said Clara Cluck. "Come and join our choir—we're practicing for a spring concert."

"No, thank you," said Donald Duck. "I'm taking my alarm clock in for repairs. It isn't loud enough."

"Huh!" snorted Clara. "What a silly excuse!" And she huffed away to choir practice.

"Poor Unca Donald!" giggled his nephews. "He can never wake up in the morning!"

"He especially wants to wake up on time tomorrow," said Huey, "because Daisy Duck is going shopping and he's hoping to meet her."

Dewey had a bright idea. "Choir practice outside his window would wake him!" he said.

"Gosh, yes!" agreed Louie. "Let's ask Clara Cluck!"

They rushed after the musical hen and asked their question in a rather careful way.

"Fancy Unca Donald not singing!"

"Mean!"

"Serve him right if the choir did its practice *right outside his window*!"

"So it would!" chortled Clara.

The next morning Donald was awakened by loud

56

singing. "Hooray!" he shouted, as he jumped out of bed. "That silly hen has done me a favor! I'm in plenty of time to meet Daisy Duck at the bus stop. What a lovely surprise for her!"

He waited for ages at the bus stop. Bus after bus went by, but no Daisy. At last Donald went home again—and who should he see but Daisy Duck, singing in the choir! "I thought you were going shopping!" he spluttered.

"I changed my mind," said Daisy sweetly. "You should join our choir, Donald—we need a tenor."

"I will," babbled Donald. "I'll join at once!"

The next morning Donald's nephews saw Daisy setting out shopping.

"Unca Donald," they shouted, "wake up! Run and get the bus! Daisy's going shopping!"

"That's what you said yesterday," yawned Donald. "But thanks for waking me, boys. I'll be in heaps of time for choir practice."

"But, Unca Donald—" began his nephews.

"Go *away*!" shouted Donald.

He arrived at choir practice with a big bunch of flowers—but Daisy wasn't there.

"Oh, Donald!" gushed Clara Cluck, "for me? I didn't know you cared!"

And the whole choir giggled!

The Red Plastic Rain Hat

Minnie Mouse wanted to go out, but it looked like rain. She put her coat on and said to herself, "Where's my rain hat?" She had a very nice red plastic rain hat with colored flowers on it. She looked on the hall stand and found her sun bonnet and her yachting cap and her driving cap and her woolly skiing cap—but no rain hat.

"That's funny," she muttered. "Perhaps I put it in my dresser." She ran upstairs and searched through her dresser. She found her spangled evening dress and her two-piece bathing suit, her tweed hunting jacket and her crimson velvet riding habit—but no rain hat.

"Did I put it in my hanky drawer?" she wondered. She opened the drawer and found her ostrich-feather fan and her gypsy earrings and her powder-blue bedsocks and her five-yards-long string of artificial pearls—but no rain hat.

"I can't have put it in the shoe rack," she frowned. In the shoe rack she found her rubber boots, her fluffy slippers, her pink satin dancing pumps and her wooden-soled arch-supporting sandals—but no rain hat.

"I bet Pluto's got it!" she exclaimed—and ran to Pluto's basket. She found nine old bones, a chewed rubber ball and half a slipper—but no rain hat.

"I'll just have to go without it, then," she sighed. It was raining hard now, so she took her umbrella with her. When she opened it something soft fell out on to her head, and it was—yes!—the red plastic rain hat!

Who Won?

Mowgli decided to have a track meet. He explained to all the animals what a race was, and told them about things like Throwing the Discus and Putting the Shot. Then they started.

The only trouble was, the animals were not very good at keeping to the rules. The monkeys decided that it was more fun to throw peanuts than a javelin, and several people got hit in the eye. The egg-and-spoon race was run without any spoons—you don't find spoons in a jungle—and was won by a bird who flew very quickly to the winning post, where she *laid* an egg!

Mowgli was rather cross. "This is a silly track meet," he grumbled. "Nobody does anything properly. Just look at the Cross-Country Race—everyone's running in different directions!"

"That doesn't matter," said Bagheera. "A race is to find out who runs quickest. Never mind *where* they run."

"I think a race is to see who gets there first," objected Baloo, frowning.

Merlin: "Does the water always come through the roof like this?"
Madam Mim: "Oh no, only when it rains."

60

"Rubbish!" snapped Bagheera. "I run faster than you. Right? So I *must* get there first!"

"You might not," said Baloo darkly. "Let's arrange a race, and we'll see."

"Good idea!" said Mowgli. He marked out a course in a huge circle that went right round the jungle and ended where it began. Bagheera and Baloo took up their positions at the starting line and Mowgli shouted, "Ready—Set—GO!"

Bagheera set off like an express train, and disappeared along the course in a cloud of dust. Baloo, on the other hand, sat down exactly where he was. "Run, Baloo!" shouted Mowgli. "You'll never get there first!"

"I *am* here first," said Baloo calmly—and sat down at the winning post to wait for Bagheera, who soon came panting up. When he saw how he had been tricked, Bagheera was furious, but Baloo said, "I got here first, yes. But you *do* run faster than me. It just depends on what a race really is."

Mowgli, to stop the argument, said, "Remember, it's April Fool's Day and everything for fun."

Bambi's April Shower

"Don't go far away, Bambi," said his mother. "It's showery April weather and you might get very wet."

"It's lovely and sunny!" said the little deer. "It doesn't look a bit like April showers!" And he went skipping off through the forest. He didn't *mean* to go far away, but when the sun disappeared behind a black cloud he looked round for his mother and couldn't see her anywhere. Big drops of rain began to fall. Bambi wished he had taken more notice of his mother.

Suddenly he heard a cheeping noise. Looking down, he saw a baby bird crouched in the grass, cheeping miserably.

"What's the matter?" asked Bambi.

"I'm all wet," sobbed the little bird, "and I can't find my Mummy."

"I can't find mine, either," said Bambi, trying to sound grown-up, "but we'll be all right. It's only an April shower."

"I'm *not* all right," wept the little bird.

"Look," said Bambi, "there's a nice dry place under that bush. I'll creep in there and you can snuggle down beside me."

Warm and dry under the bush, the little bird cheered up. "It's nice in here," he said. "I *am* glad I met you!"

"I'm glad, too," said Bambi.

"*Are* you?" The little bird was surprised. "But you're too big to be afraid of April showers!"

"Yes," smiled Bambi. "Much too big!"

After the shower the little bird's mother came and thanked Bambi, and Bambi went back to his own mother, feeling very grown-up and pleased with himself!

Walking the Plank

Donald Duck's nephews, Huey, Dewey and Louie, saw Daisy Duck tiptoeing round a big puddle on her way out of her front garden.

"Let's put a plank across the puddle," suggested Huey. "Then she won't get her feet wet," agreed Dewey. "And she'll think Unca Donald did it!" chimed in Louie. They all smiled; Uncle Donald was always trying to make Daisy like him, and it never seemed to work.

The ducklings found a long plank and put it across the puddle. Then they heard Daisy coming back, and hid behind a bush. Daisy had met Donald, who was carrying her shopping basket. He opened the gate for her, saw the puddle, but didn't notice the plank. "Let me carry you across the puddle!" he offered gallantly—and seized Daisy, staggering a little.

"Unca Donald," hissed the ducklings, "there's a plank! LOOK!"

"Plank?" quacked Donald. "What plank? YARK!" He stepped on the edge of the plank and the other end came up like a seesaw and hit him in the eye. He dropped Daisy, who fell in the puddle, and dropped the shopping basket on top of her. There was mud everywhere, and Daisy was so cross that she hit Donald in the other eye.

"Oh, Unca Donald," wailed the ducklings, "it's all gone wrong again!" But when they explained to Daisy what they had been trying to do she smiled and turned rather pink—and invited them all in for tea.

And afterwards Donald Duck gave his nephews two cents each for their kind idea!

Banana Fritters

Huey: "Why does a
polar bear wear a
fur coat?"
Louie: "Because
he'd look silly in a
tweed one."

Mowgli was making jam with wild berries he had
picked in the jungle. All the animals came to
sniff the delicious smell.

"We're bored with bananas," chattered the monkeys.
"What else can we eat, Mowgli?"

"I don't know," said Mowgli.

"Eggs are egg-sausting," sighed Kaa, the rock snake.
"What else can I eat, Mowgli?"

"I don't know," said Mowgli.

"Nuts get mo-nut-anous," twittered the birds. "What
else can we eat, Mowgli?"

"I don't know," said Mowgli.

Then Baloo the bear padded softly up and growled
"Bears can't *bear* coconut milk. Now, think, little one,
and tell the animals what new food they can eat. The
man child is too clever to say, 'I don't know'."

"But I—" began Mowgli. Then he caught Baloo's stern

eye. The big bear was not his teacher for nothing. Mowgli thought hard. Coconut milk, nuts, eggs, bananas. Aha!

With two big stones he ground up the nuts and mixed them with beaten eggs and some coconut milk. He peeled the bananas, sliced them, and dropped them into the mixture, then fried them over his fire. He served them on palm-leaf plates, with lashings of his jungle berry jam, and they were *delicious.*

"Gorgeous!" chorused the animals. "What are they called, Mowgli?"

"I don't know!" grinned Mowgli. And this time he really *didn't* know. Baloo shut his eyes and thought. Then he opened them and said, "Banana fritters!"

And, although we make them with slightly different things, they are still called banana fritters today. Ask your mother!

65

Never a Cross Word!

Pooh Bear, out for a stroll with his friend Owl, came across Eeyore, who was staring very seriously at a large bit of paper.

"Good morning, Eeyore," said Pooh. Eeyore looked around, slowly. "Ah," he said, "Pooh. Do you know what this is?"

"Paper," said Pooh.

Eeyore sighed, "What *sort* of paper, Pooh?"

"It's a newspaper," said Owl briskly. "But I didn't know you could read, Eeyore."

Eeyore went on staring at his paper. Pooh watched, very impressed. Then Owl said, "You've got it upside down, Eeyore."

"Has he?" asked Pooh. "How do you know, Owl?"

"Because," said Owl, "there's a picture of a house, look, and it's standing on its roof. Wrong way up."

"So it is," agreed Pooh. "What's *that* picture? The one with little squares all over?"

"That," said Owl, "is a crossword. Christopher Robin said so."

Eeyore was looking gloomy. "I didn't think papers had cross words," he sighed. "What are they cross about?"

"I don't know," said Pooh.

Owl laughed, "Not angry-cross, Eeyore," he said kindly. "Just crisscross. Look, like this." And with one claw he traced a cross in the earth.

"What's that got to do with the little squares?" asked Pooh.

"Dear, dear, dear," tutted Owl, "you *are* dim, Pooh. You put a crisscross in each of the little squares. Christopher Robin showed me."

"Put a crisscross *how*?" asked Pooh, puzzled. Then they all jumped as Christopher Robin's voice suddenly broke in. "With a pencil, you sillies!" He had arrived unnoticed, and luckily had his pencil case with him. He gave Pooh a red pencil, Owl a green one and Eeyore a purple one. Christopher Robin had a thick black pen and they had a lovely time filling in crisscrosses on the crossword.

When it was all finished and they were walking home for lunch, Pooh whispered, "Christopher Robin—is that really how they do crosswords?"

"There are other ways," Christopher Robin whispered back, "but they're much more difficult than yours. And not nearly so pretty!"

Pooh sighed happily. "Then *that's* all right," he said.

Pluto's Bone

Pluto had a big, meaty bone. He chewed at it for a long time, then looked for somewhere safe to hide it. He started to dig a hole in the garden but Minnie banged on the window and shouted, "Pluto! Stop that!" She came storming out. "That's my flowerbed! *Bad* dog! Bury your beastly bone somewhere else!"

Pluto's ears went down. He picked up his bone and slunk off with his tail between his legs, as Minnie went inside and banged the door. "Where is the right place to bury a bone?" Pluto wondered. He wasn't allowed to dig holes in the lawn or in the flowerbed. He came to the trash can outside the back door and pricked up his ears. Ideal! A nice, safe place to put his bone while he found a proper place to hide it. He popped his bone into the trash can and bustled out of the back gate to look for a good hiding place.

Professor von Drake: "Where was the Magna Carta signed?" **Wart:** "At the bottom."

Pluto was halfway down the road when a truck arrived, and the trash men started carrying the cans out to empty them. With a loud yelp, Pluto rushed back —but, too late! His bone, along with the other rubbish, was tipped into the truck, which then drove away! Pluto galloped after it, barking loudly. The truck drove faster, and soon Pluto was left far behind. He gave one last yap, then sat down on the pavement and howled. He howled so loudly that windows rattled and babies cried, and several cars skidded to a halt because they thought it was a police siren!

Pluto was howling right outside a butcher's shop and the noise he made was so awful that all the customers in the shop ran out without stopping to buy anything. The butcher came out, red-faced and cross, with a huge, juicy bone in his hand. "Here," he shouted, "take this and howl somewhere else!"

Pluto stopped howling and grinned instead. Then he ran all the way home with his delicious new bone. If anything happened to this one, he thought happily, he knew exactly how to get another!

Cold Head

A cold wind was blowing, and Uncle Scrooge, who was hanging some twice-used tea bags on the line to dry, felt chilly. He stuffed some more newspapers down his trouser legs and buttoned up his grandfather's jacket more tightly, but he still felt cold.

"It's my head," he muttered. "There's not enough hair on it. Bother!"

Being so mean, Uncle Scrooge never thought of buying a hat. He went indoors and started looking for something to keep his head warm. He found an old tablecloth and wrapped it around his head—and at that moment the mail came. Uncle Scrooge opened his letter. "'Free Offer!'" he read. "'Try on a lovely wig at Horace's Hairstyles.' Free! Aha!" And the old miser scuttled off to Horace's Hairstyles, still wearing his tablecloth.

Horace Horsecollar thought Uncle Scrooge was a lady. "Good morning, madam," he said. "You would like to try a wig?"

"Yes, please," said Scrooge. "Free!"

"It costs nothing to *try*!" smiled Horace.

Scrooge tried on wig after wig: long, flowing wigs; short, curly wigs; black wigs; yellow wigs; red wigs. "They are all very nice and warm," he said. "I think I'll have this brown one with ringlets."

"That one is ten dollars, madam," said Horace.

"What?" spluttered Uncle Scrooge. "But it said Free!"

"Free to *try*!" grinned Horace. "Not to *buy*!"

"How mean," sulked Uncle Scrooge. And he put his tablecloth back on his head and went home.

"It may not be pretty," he muttered, "but at least it's free!"

Ears at Stake!

"What a windy day!" gasped the March Hare. "It's blowing so hard that my ears are flying out sideways. I do wish I could get them to stand up straight!"

Looking over the Mad Hatter's garden fence, he saw a pile of nice thin stakes. "Just the thing!" he chortled. He hopped in, took two stakes and tied one to each ear with green garden twine. "There!" he crowed. "Much more comfortable! Ears up again!" He found a sheltered corner by the greenhouse, sat down with his back against the wall and was soon fast asleep.

Along came the Mad Hatter and the Dormouse. They went into the greenhouse and planted lots of geraniums in flowerpots. The Dormouse began to yawn as usual and the Mad Hatter said, "You need some fresh air to wake you up! Take these pots outside and put a stake in each one, to hold the plants nice and steady."

The Dormouse trotted outside with two flowerpots but the fresh air made him sleepier still. Eyes half shut, he put the pots down on either side of the March Hare and staked each plant firmly—but the stakes he used were the ones attached to the March Hare's long ears!

"Help!" shrieked the March Hare, waking up. "My ears! What's happened? Heavy weights! Can't get up!" But although the March Hare was making a tremendous noise the Dormouse didn't hear him. He had curled up and gone to sleep right at the March Hare's feet, and nothing would wake him.

"Wake up, stupid!" screamed the March Hare, poking the Dormouse with his toe. "You've planted my ears!" But it was the Mad Hatter who came to his rescue. He untied the March Hare's ears, then said, "It serves you right for stealing my stakes!"

"I didn't steal them," protested the March Hare, "I just *borrowed* them!" He explained his difficulty with the wind and the Mad Hatter said, "Come into the greenhouse. There's no wind in there."

"Oh, *thank* you!" said the March Hare.

"Thank *you!*" grinned the Mad Hatter. "Since the Dormouse is asleep, *you* can help me plant my geraniums!"

71

Sneezing Powder

Bernard and Bianca, the intrepid little mice from the International Rescue Aid Society, found themselves outside a Joke Shop one day. The window was full of things like Plastic Ink Blots and Horrible Hairy Spiders, and Bernard saw a box labeled Sneezing Powder. "That could come in useful," he said—and bought some. When he came out of the shop, Evinrude the dragonfly whizzed up. "Quick!" he gasped. "Madame Medusa is planning a jewel robbery. A carload of henchmen is calling for her in half an hour. What can we do?"

"First—get to the Pawn Shop Boutique," said Bianca. Arriving, they sneaked in through a mousehole and Bernard emptied his box of sneezing powder into the powder bowl on Madame Medusa's dressing table. He slid the lid back on just in time, as Madame Medusa came in. "A-thieving we will go!" she sang as she put on her slinkiest gown. "A-thieving—" There was a knock at the door. "Coming!" she called—and powdered her nose liberally before going out.

She got into the car with the henchmen, rubbing her nose hard. Then she began to sneeze. "Oo-ooph!" she spluttered, waving her hanky and spreading the powder all over the car. "Whatever's the matter with my nose? Aa-tschoo!"

The watching mice saw the car start, veer from side to side, then stop. Everyone in it was sneezing too hard to see a thing! A policeman approached, notebook in hand, and Bianca giggled. "Bang goes the jewel robbery! The sneezing powder *did* come in useful, didn't it?"

Top Hat

"**W**here's your Easter bonnet, Clarabelle?" asked Clara Cluck. "We're all looking smart for the Easter Parade—even Horace Horsecollar has got a daisy in his straw hat."

"I did have a hat somewhere," said Clarabelle. "Now, where did I put it?"

She hunted about, and found her hat in the barn, squashed flat. "Botheration," she muttered, "I must have sat on it."

"All line up!" crowed the rooster from the barn roof. "In the meadow, straight away!"

"Mustn't be late," squawked Clara Cluck. "Come along, all!" She put her dandelion flower bonnet straight and bustled off.

Poor Clarabelle followed the others. She was the only animal in the whole farmyard without an Easter bonnet. She felt so bad about it that she didn't go into the meadow with the others. She just peeped through the hedge instead.

"Off we go!" cackled Clara Cluck, and the parade began. The geese looked very pretty in cherry blossom berets, and the pigs wore smart yellow topknots made of plaited buttercups. The sheep came next, but Clarabelle

Geppetto: "Why do white sheep eat more grass than black sheep?"
Pinocchio: "Because there are more of them."

couldn't see them properly through the hedge. She pushed a little hole in it, but the hedge was thick with pink blossoms and it was very prickly. She tried a bit farther along, but there it was full of wild roses and they were even more prickly!

At last Clarabelle found a gap and pushed her head right through. She heard a loud chirping noise but she was too interested in the parade to take any notice.

Everyone noticed Clarabelle, though!

"Oh!" they gasped. "Just *look* at Clarabelle's bonnet!"

"Clarabelle," said Horace Horsecollar, "you look beautiful. Pink blossoms round your horns and red roses behind your ears, and a bird's nest on top of your head with four little birds in it! I reckon you deserve first prize!"

"Hear, hear!" shouted all the animals. So Clarabelle was given first prize.

Clarabelle blushed. "Thank you all very much," she said.

"However did you think of it?" asked Horace.

Clarabelle blushed even more. "It just sort of *came* to me," she mooed.

And nobody knew how true that was!

Dumbo and the Flying Trapeze

D umbo had always dreamed of having a go on the flying trapeze. "I can fly," he pointed out, "so I wouldn't get hurt."

But the family of trapeze artists wouldn't hear of it. "Iss too dangerous," said Mother. "You haf no practice," said Father. "We are *experts*," ended their son fiercely. Their little daughter smiled at Dumbo but her mother said, "Go and practice your handsprings!" So that was that.

But one day when Father was hammering in a tent peg he accidentally hammered his toe instead. It swelled up and turned bright blue. "I shall never hang by my feet tonight," he groaned. "Never mind," soothed his wife, "the children and I can manage." But that afternoon when she was sewing spangles on a new costume, Mother accidentally put her fingers through the sewing machine. "Ow!" she shrieked. "I shall never hang by my hands tonight!"

"Don't worry," soothed her son. "We shall manage without you." But when he was taking an afternoon nap

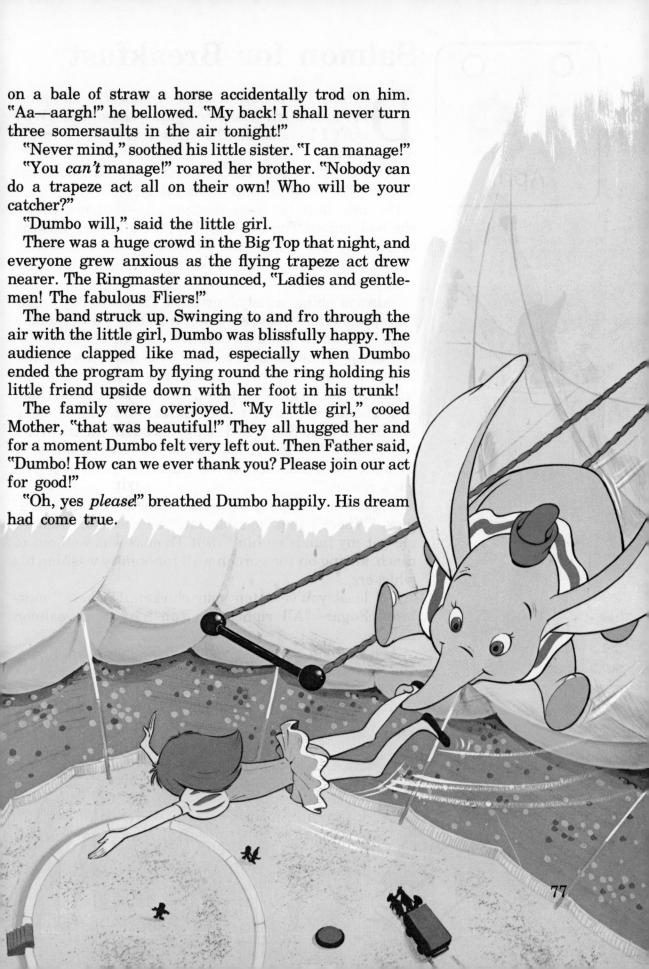

on a bale of straw a horse accidentally trod on him. "Aa—aargh!" he bellowed. "My back! I shall never turn three somersaults in the air tonight!"

"Never mind," soothed his little sister. "I can manage!"

"You *can't* manage!" roared her brother. "Nobody can do a trapeze act all on their own! Who will be your catcher?"

"Dumbo will," said the little girl.

There was a huge crowd in the Big Top that night, and everyone grew anxious as the flying trapeze act drew nearer. The Ringmaster announced, "Ladies and gentlemen! The fabulous Fliers!"

The band struck up. Swinging to and fro through the air with the little girl, Dumbo was blissfully happy. The audience clapped like mad, especially when Dumbo ended the program by flying round the ring holding his little friend upside down with her foot in his trunk!

The family were overjoyed. "My little girl," cooed Mother, "that was beautiful!" They all hugged her and for a moment Dumbo felt very left out. Then Father said, "Dumbo! How can we ever thank you? Please join our act for good!"

"Oh, yes *please!*" breathed Dumbo happily. His dream had come true.

77

Salmon for Breakfast

Duchess, the beautiful white Aristocat, didn't want her breakfast. "Chicken again," she sighed. "Why can't I have salmon? I know there's some in the refrigerator."

"You finish up that chicken first," scolded Edgar the butler. "I'm tired of your wasteful ways."

Duchess shut her eyes disdainfully—but not before she had noticed Thomas O'Malley, the alley cat, lurking outside by the trash can. "Thomas," she murmured, "could you possibly eat this boring old chicken for me? I really *couldn't.*"

"Always oblige a lady," grinned Thomas—but Edgar had spotted him and rushed out, furiously waving a dish mop. "Get out, you nasty common cat!" he shouted. "Go on—shoo!" Thomas leapt nimbly over the trash can but kicked off the lid as he went. Clumsy Edgar trod on the trash can lid, tripped, and fell head first into the trash can. Thomas O'Malley nipped quickly into the kitchen, and by the time Edgar had struggled out of the trash can the chicken had gone. "Delicious!" beamed Thomas. "I thought you'd like it," purred Duchess. "Look out—Edgar's coming!"

Edgar was dripping with tea leaves and potato peelings. "Where's that horrible cat?" he shouted. "Just let me get my hands on him!" But Thomas was well out of reach, sitting on the garden wall innocently washing his whiskers.

"At least you've eaten your chicken, Duchess," muttered Edgar. "All right—you can have some salmon now."

And as soon as Edgar went off to clean himself up, Duchess and Thomas shared a second breakfast!

Pluto's Barking Day

Pluto was having a barking day. He barked at the daffodils, and he barked at the wind, and he barked at the clouds in the sky. He barked at his breakfast, and he barked at the milkman, and he barked so loudly at the trash men that they didn't dare come in and get the trash. "That dog's dangerous," they said.

Mickey Mouse had to carry the trash can down to the truck, and he was rather annoyed about it. "Why are you making all that silly noise, Pluto?" he scolded. "Perhaps you need exercise. I'm taking Minnie to the Echo Cave this afternoon. You'd better come, too."

Pluto thought this was a lovely idea and barked even louder, and Mickey went indoors with his fingers in his ears. Pluto went on barking until they set out for the Echo Cave, and he barked all the way there. At the entrance to the cave Mickey said, "Now, Pluto, please don't bark in here. You're annoying everyone." Pluto grinned and wagged his tail, and they went in.

Once inside the Echo Cave, Pluto got so excited that he forgot what Mickey had said. "Bow-wow-wow!" he barked. But poor Pluto didn't know about the echo. It answered him with a tremendous BOW-WOW-WOW! which sounded like a pack of elephant-sized hounds. Pluto turned and fled.

Mickey and Minnie laughed and laughed, and the Echo Cave laughed even louder. Pluto could hear it all the way home, and he didn't bark for nearly half an hour!

Walking on Air

Jasper: "Waiter! My boiled egg is bad!"
Tony: "Don't blame me, sir—I only laid the table."

Princess Aurora was reading a story. Suddenly she looked up. "What does 'walking on air' mean?" she asked. "It means you are very happy," explained Merryweather. "So you feel all springy and light-footed." Aurora nodded, and went on reading.

After lunch the fairy godmothers wanted to go and pick blackberries. "That sounds lovely," said Aurora, who had finished her story. So they took baskets and hooked sticks for reaching high branches, and set out.

They found heaps of blackberries and soon their baskets were full. A splash of rain on Aurora's face made her look up. Black clouds had gathered. "Oh, dear!" she cried. "It's going to rain and all our lovely blackberries will get wet."

"So will our feet," said Flora, who was wearing her favorite pink slippers. "*And* our hair!" said Fauna, who had spent the morning curling her ringlets.

"I'm sure the trees will help us," said Merryweather. She waved her wand, and the trees bent their branches over to make a leafy roof. It rained very hard, but not a drop came through to dampen blackberries, slippers or hair.

When the storm was over, Aurora thanked the trees for their help and they set out for home—but the fields were soaking wet. "What was it your story said, Aurora?" asked Merryweather. "'Walking on air'? What a good idea!" And in a twinkle of a wand they were dancing along a foot above the ground.

"Now I *really* understand what 'walking on air' means!" laughed Aurora. "What a beautiful feeling!"

Very Special Honey

Christopher Robin was reading what it said on one of Pooh's honey pots. "'Very Special Honey,'" he read, "'made by English Wild Bees.'"

"You are *clever*, Christopher Robin," said Pooh.

"Some of us are," said Christopher Robin carelessly, "and some aren't."

"I'm not," said Pooh. "I am a bear of very little brain." Then he thought of something. "Christopher Robin —what is an English Wild Bee?"

"It lives in England," said Christopher Robin, "and it's a bee . . . and it's—er—wild. Not tame."

"Is it dangerous?" asked Pooh nervously.

"It might be," said Christopher Robin. "You never know with bees. I must go now, Pooh. Good-bye!"

"Time for a little something," murmured Pooh, when Christopher Robin had gone. He opened his pot of Very Special Honey made by English Wild Bees and took a big spoonful. "M'm! Delicious!"

Suddenly there was a loud buzzing noise. A bee had come in through the open window. Another one came,

and then another—and they all made for Pooh's pot of
Very Special Honey. Pooh put the lid on quickly and hid
the pot behind his back, but the bees seemed to know
where it was. They buzzed round him angrily. "Perhaps
these are English Wild Bees," Pooh said to himself. "Not
tame." He felt rather scared. "Go away!" he told the bees
firmly. But they took no notice.

Pooh took his pot of Very Special Honey into the
pantry and put it on the shelf. Several bees came, too.
There was an open honey pot on the shelf, too. The honey
had all been eaten but somehow the pot hadn't got
washed. The bees seemed to think there was plenty in
the empty pot for them and clustered around it happily.
Pooh had a good idea. He carried the empty pot outside,
and when all the bees were busy around it he went in
again and shut all the doors and windows. Then he got
out his pot of Very Special Honey and settled down to
enjoy it without the English Wild Bees.

For a bear of very little brain, he thought happily, he
managed quite well, really!

Donald the Brave!

Donald Duck was talking to Daisy in the garden, and his three nephews were listening from their bedroom window.

"I'm so brave!" Donald was boasting. "I'd rescue you from a burning building—I'd save your life if you were drowning—and if you were attacked by a man-eating tiger I'd beat it off single-handed, like this! BANG! BANG!"

"Oh, Donald," breathed Daisy, "you are wonderful!"

"Unca Donald's doing all right," whispered Huey.

"She thinks he's marvelous," nodded Dewey.

Louie looked thoughtful. "It would be even better if Unca Donald could *prove* how brave he is," he said. "Now, if we got the tiger-skin rug from the sitting room . . ."

". . . and put it on!" agreed Huey excitedly . . .

". . . Unca Donald could *show* Daisy how brave he is!" chimed in Louie.

The three ducklings draped themselves in the tiger-skin rug and prowled out into the garden, growling.

84

"Help!" screamed Daisy. "A man-eating tiger! Aargh!" And she fainted clean away. As for Donald, he took to his heels and fled down the garden, then scrambled up to the top of the tallest tree he could find and sat there, shaking.

The ducklings came out from the tiger skin and called, "Unca Donald! It's only us! We wanted you to show Daisy how brave you are!"

Donald came down from his tree, very red in the face. "Thought I'd carry Daisy to safety," he muttered. "Silly girl didn't come. Where is she? Oh!"

Daisy's eyelashes were fluttering. "Quick!" said the ducklings. "She's coming to! Put your foot on the tiger's head, Unca Donald—you'll still look very brave!"

"Right," said Donald. As Daisy opened her eyes she saw Donald looking masterful, with his arms folded and one foot on the tiger's head. *And* she saw the ducklings.

"Fancy needing three little boys to help you!" she snorted. "Call yourself brave! I'm going home!"

"But I *am* brave!" blustered Donald. "Daisy—wait!"

"Poor Unca Donald!" sighed the ducklings. "There are some people you just *can't* help!"

Hiawatha and the Wolf

Little Hiawatha was washing his trousers in the stream. When they were clean he looked around for somewhere to hang them up to dry. The trees were too high for him to reach, but he found a bush with some nice bare branches sticking up from it. Just the thing! Hiawatha hung his trousers on a branch.

At that moment the wolf came snarling up. Little Hiawatha hid behind a tree and, peeping around, saw his trousers and the branch they were hung on leap up and gallop away! The branch was not a branch at all—it was the antlers of a stag which had been dozing behind the bush.

The wolf rushed after the stag and little Hiawatha rushed after the wolf. "Bring back my trousers!" he shouted. The stag, startled by Hiawatha's voice, jerked his head up, and the trousers sailed through the air and landed—*plonk!*—right over the wolf's head. He couldn't see a thing.

"Help! Grr-wow!" howled the wolf. "Let me go!" Little Hiawatha roared with laughter, and even the stag stopped running and giggled nervously. The wolf seemed to think Hiawatha's trousers were a very big, fierce animal. Little Hiawatha crept close to the wolf and growled, "I am King Tiger. Leave my friends alone or I will squash you flat!"

"Anything you say," whined the wolf, "only let me go!" And he slunk off into the woods. Little Hiawatha pulled his trousers off the wolf as he went. "Whew!" he gasped. "Next time I'll make sure my bush *is* a bush!"

86

Frocks and Flowers

One day, Princess Aurora was out for a walk with two of her fairy godmothers, Flora and Fauna. Merryweather, her other godmother, had gone shopping.

Aurora, Flora and Fauna sat down to rest on some springy grass where lots of bluebells grew. Aurora picked one of the blue flowers and gazed at it. "What a beautiful color!" she said. "As blue as a summer sky. And such a pretty shape, too, curving out at the edge. I wish I could wear a bluebell as a dress!"

"Do you really?" asked Flora.

"Really and truly?" added Fauna.

Aurora nodded. "Really and truly," she said. And— zing! There she was, in a bluebell dress with real petals. "Oh, darling godmothers!" she cried. "Thank you *so* much!"

She danced all the way home in her bluebell dress —but by the time they arrived her petals were beginning to wilt, and the lovely azure blue was fading to blotchy gray.

When Merryweather came back from shopping, Princess Aurora was in tears. Merryweather knew why. "Don't cry, my dear," she said. "Look what I've bought you." And from out of her basket she drew a length of azure blue fabric, as light as bluebell petals and as strong as spider silk. "I'll make you a dress," she said. And—ping! Aurora was wearing a new and lovelier bluebell dress.

"That's better," said Merryweather. "Only plants can wear flowers."

"Yes," agreed Aurora. "But how did you know I wanted a bluebell dress?"

Merryweather smiled. "Magic, of course," she said.

87

Sticky Bud Stamp

Donald Duck: "Did you hear the story of the broken pencil? There's no point to it."

"Pooh, will you be a postman for me?" said Christopher Robin. "This is a letter to Owl. Can you put it through his door?"

"Yes," said Pooh. He stared at the letter as he set out towards Owl's house. He thought letters should have a colored bit of paper stuck on one corner—a stamp, they called it. This letter didn't have a stamp.

Pooh took the letter home and cut out a square from a blue honey-pot label. That was a good stamp. But how to stick it on? Honey was too nice to waste as glue. Pooh saw some sticky buds on a chestnut tree, conveniently low. Just the thing! He rubbed his stamp with a sticky bud and stuck it, rather messily, on the letter. Then he went to Owl's house.

Owl opened his letter and stared at the writing. Pooh stared, too. "What does it say?" he asked. "Er—I haven't got my glasses on," said Owl. "Then put them on," suggested Pooh. "I can't see to find them," said Owl. "Not without my glasses."

Christopher Robin arrived. "You got my letter, then?" he said. "What's the answer?" "I don't know," said Owl. Pooh looked worried. "Didn't I mail it properly?" he asked. "I put a stamp on it—look!"

Christopher Robin laughed. "You mailed it *beautifully*!" he said. "And it says, 'Come for a picnic this afternoon, everyone'!"

"Thank you, Christopher Robin," said Owl. "We'll come."

"Yes, *thank* you!" beamed Pooh.

Christopher Robin laughed. "Thank *you*, Pooh!" he said.

Waste Not . . .

Thomas O'Malley was hungry. Being an alley cat, he had to wait for meals to turn up. And nothing had turned up for quite some time.

Through an open window a beautiful smell reached Thomas's nose—one of his favorite smells. It was roast mutton, cooling a bit so that the fat was setting around the edge of the plate. Delicious! Thomas jumped onto the windowsill.

Sitting at the table was a little boy, looking cross and miserable. The plate in front of him had two or three bits of cold, fatty meat on it. Thomas licked his lips. "I don't want it!" pouted the little boy. His mother frowned. "No apple pie if you don't eat your meat," she said. "I can't bear waste." Then she went over to the kitchen sink and clattered the dishes about.

Thomas seized his chance and jumped in through the window. He rubbed around the little boy's legs and looked hungry—which was easy as he *was* hungry. "Here!" whispered the little boy. "Quick!" He handed the bits of meat down to Thomas, who chewed them up with great enjoyment. He was just finishing the last one when the little boy's mother saw him.

"Oh!" she cried. "You beastly cat! You've eaten my little boy's dinner!" Thomas jumped back through the window, taking his bit of meat with him.

"It wasn't wasted, Mom!" grinned the little boy. "So can I have some apple pie?"

"I suppose so," sighed his mother.

Thomas O'Malley washed his whiskers, smiling. Wasted, indeed! No such thing!

Traffic Lights

Captain Hook:
"You're late—you should have been here at nine o'clock!"
Mr. Smee: "Why, what happened?"

"Let's go shopping," said Merryweather, "by car!" And in a twinkle of her magic wand there stood a splendid limousine, painted bright mauve. With Flora and Fauna in the back, Merryweather set out for the big town. All went well until they came to red traffic lights.

"Silly things," muttered Merryweather. "Time for a change!" And with a flick of her magic wand she changed the lights green and drove across the crossroads. Unfortunately the other lights were still at green, too, and there were terrible honkings of horns and screamings of brakes as angry motorists jammed to a halt.

A policeman held up his hand. "You have just crossed a red light, madam," he said. "No, I didn't!" said Merryweather innocently. "Look!" Sure enough, all the lights were still at green and the traffic was in a dreadful muddle. The policeman rushed to sort it out, and Merryweather drove on, chuckling.

The fairy godmothers had a lovely morning's shopping. On their way home, though, they came to a tremendous traffic jam. "The lights have gone wrong!" shouted another driver. "We'll be here for hours!"

"These lights seem to be bewitched," groaned the policeman, mopping his brow.

"Perhaps I can help!" suggested Merryweather, and with a flick of her wand the lights were working perfectly again.

"Oh, *thank* you, madam!" said the policeman with a gasp of relief, as the traffic started to move again. "However did you do that?"

"I'm just naturally helpful!" smiled Merryweather, and drove on home.

Yellow Paint

Donald Duck was painting the bedroom floor a nice bright yellow. He started at the door with a wide stripe and dipped his brush into the pot again.

His nephews, Huey, Dewey and Louie, came upstairs to see what he was doing. They stared at the yellow paint and then stared at each other.

"Unca Donald——" began Huey. Donald flapped his brush impatiently. "Don't interrupt me, boys," he said. "You can see I'm busy."

"Yes," agreed Dewey, "but you've started at the door."

"Good place to start," said Donald, painting busily.

The ducklings looked at each other and Louie asked, "But how——"

"Don't waste time with silly questions," interrupted Donald. "I want to get this done. Daisy is coming round at four o'clock."

"But, Unca Donald!" wailed the ducklings.

"Go away!" shouted Donald. So his nephews went.

Grumpy: "That's a ridiculous pair of socks you're wearing—they don't match."
Doc: "I know. And the funny thing is, I've got another pair at home exactly like these!"

At four o'clock Daisy Duck rang the bell. "Coming, dear!" shouted Donald—and then he saw that he couldn't reach the door except by walking across his wet, yellow-painted floor. He glanced out of the window. No, it was too far to jump.

"What are you doing up there, Donald?" called Daisy.

"Er—resting," said Donald. "I've got a sudden headache. Better stay here, I think."

"Huh!" snorted Daisy, stalking off. Donald heard her call, "Hallo, Gladstone! *You* haven't got a headache, have you?" And then, to his fury, he saw her walking down the road arm in arm with Gladstone Gander.

"Poor Unca Donald!" giggled his nephews. "But we *did* try to tell him!"

A Narrow Squeak

One evening the two little mice from the International Rescue Aid Society, Bernard and Bianca, were on a routine mission to check up on the wicked Madame Medusa and make sure she was up to no mischief. They approached the Pawn Shop Boutique by their usual secret mouse route, but at the hole in the baseboard where they usually went in, Bernard suddenly stopped, his sensitive nose twitching.

"What is it?" asked Bianca, behind him.

"Cheese," said Bernard.

"Do be careful," urged Bianca. "You know what our training taught us; where there is cheese, there may be traps."

Very cautiously, the two mice edged around the delicious-smelling lump of cheese and the little wooden platform it stood on. "It *is* a trap!" hissed Bianca. "Look—see the spring and the lever that comes down, bang!"

"Nasty," agreed Bernard. "What shall we do with it?"

They stared at the trap thoughtfully. "Can we move it, do you think?" wondered Bianca. "If we put it somewhere else, Madame Medusa won't be expecting it——"

"And it might trap her instead of us!" chimed in Bernard. "Let's try!"

Inch by inch, the mice nudged the trap away from the hole, and then, to their horror, they heard Madame Medusa coming. "Hide!" gasped Bianca. They dived into a half-open drawer full of chiffon scarves, perfumes and old lipsticks and, peeping out, saw that Madame Medusa was holding a fabulous necklace, glittering with precious stones.

"Ah!" gloated Madame Medusa. "You pretty little trinket!" She put the necklace down on the dressing table, and Bernard, with reckless courage, leaped out of the drawer, hurled himself at the necklace and knocked it to the floor. Quick-thinking Bianca trundled it towards the mousehole, but Madame Medusa seized a hairbrush and raised it to flatten Bianca.

"Look out!" yelled Bernard, and Madame Medusa, turning to grab him, put her fingers in the mousetrap. *Bang!*

"YOW!" yelled the wicked woman, as the mice scuttled safely down their hole again.

"That," grinned Bianca, "is what you might call a narrow squeak!"

97

Kite Rescue

Dumbo and his friend Timothy Mouse were out for a walk one windy day when they met a little girl. She was holding a big ball of string, and she was crying most bitterly.

"What's the matter?" asked Dumbo kindly.

"My kite," sobbed the little girl. "It's gone into a tree and the string's broken and I'll never get it down, *ever*."

"Yes, you will," soothed Dumbo. "Just watch." And, spreading his enormous ears, he flew up to the treetop where the kite was caught in the branches. The little girl was so amazed to see an elephant fly that she quite forgot to cry any more. But Dumbo couldn't disentangle the kite string from the branches and he flew down again.

"Don't worry," he said quickly, before the little girl could start to cry again, "I've only come for Timothy."

"Timothy?" The little girl hadn't seen Dumbo's tiny friend and she was even more amazed to see Dumbo pick up the mouse in his trunk and fly up to the top of the tree again. This time Timothy's neat little fingers soon had the kite string freed from the branches and Dumbo flew down to earth again with Timothy and the kite.

"Oh, *thank* you!" beamed the little girl. "Now I'll fly it again!"

"Mind the tree this time!" warned Dumbo.

"But it's such fun seeing you get it down!" chuckled the little girl.

"Dumbo," whispered Timothy, "shall we go on with our walk?"

"I think we'd better," Dumbo whispered back. And the little girl was so happy with her kite that she didn't even see them go.

98

Spring is Sprung

Goofy had a package of seeds. "'Very—quick —growing'," he read. "'You—will—be——'. Hey, Pluto, what does this say?"

Pluto came out of the house holding a feather duster, and looked at Goofy's seed package. He was not much better at reading than Goofy was. "'As—ton—ished'," he spelt out. "That means very, very surprised, I think." And he went indoors to carry on with his spring cleaning.

Goofy raked the garden smooth and planted his seeds. "I will be—what was it?—very, very surprised. I wonder how?" Then he gave a big yawn. Planting the seeds had made him tired. He lay down in the sunshine and soon he was fast asleep. He didn't see the gray clouds come over the sun and he didn't see Pluto come out with a bunch of rather dusty plastic flowers.

Pluto looked at his flowers and looked at the sky. "It's going to rain!" he grinned. "Hooray! It can wash my flowers!" He stuck the plastic flowers in the garden, just where Goofy had planted his seeds. Then he bustled off to finish his spring cleaning.

When it started to rain, Goofy woke up. "Whuff!" he spluttered, rubbing his eyes. "I'm wet!"

Then he saw the flowers and jumped to his feet. "Hey!" he shouted. "Pluto! Look, my flowers have grown! Pluto—what's so funny?"

But Pluto was laughing too much to answer.

"That seed package was right," went on Goofy. "I *am*—what was it?"

"Astonished," spluttered Pluto. "Look!"

"Plastic flowers!" gawped Goofy. "What *clever* seeds!"

99

The Banana Skin

Little Hiawatha was walking along a path through the pine forest one morning, eating a banana. When he had finished it he tossed the skin away, but then, on second thought, he bent and picked it up. "A banana skin is a slippery thing," he thought. "Somebody else coming along the path might slip up over it and hurt themselves."

So, swinging his banana skin and whistling a tune, Little Hiawatha continued on his way to the pond for a swim. There was a big stone in the middle of the path leading to the pond. It was quite easy to walk around the stone, but anyone absentminded or fumble-footed was bound to stub his toe on it. Little Hiawatha was much too wary a forest dweller to stub *his* toe, and he always laughed when a howl of rage and a loud splash announced that the big stone had claimed another victim. (Anyone stubbing his toe hard enough usually pitched headlong into the pond. Splash!)

Happy: "My brother had to leave his job. He was seeing spots in front of his eyes."
Sleepy: "What was his job?"
Happy: "Washing leopards at the zoo."

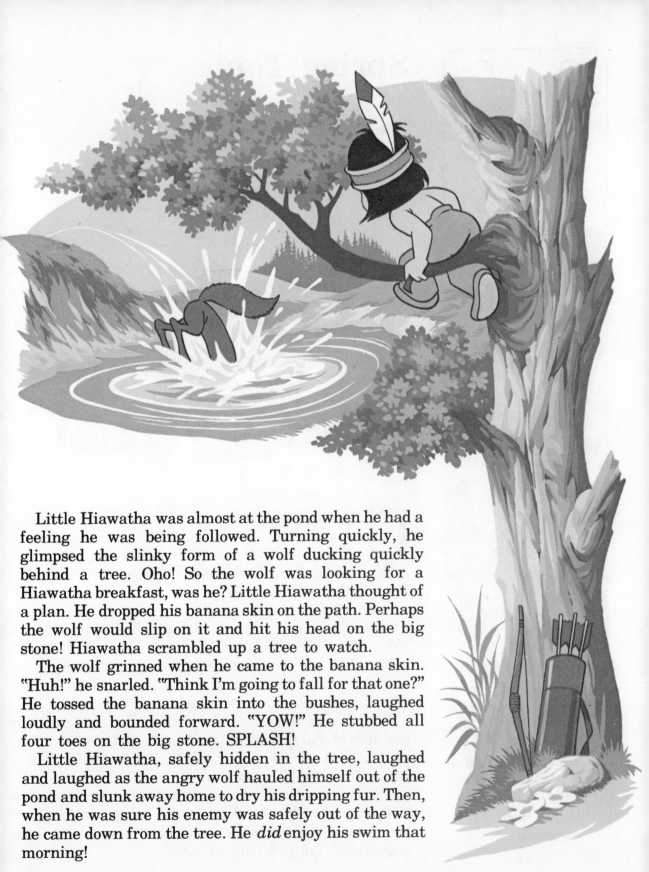

Little Hiawatha was almost at the pond when he had a feeling he was being followed. Turning quickly, he glimpsed the slinky form of a wolf ducking quickly behind a tree. Oho! So the wolf was looking for a Hiawatha breakfast, was he? Little Hiawatha thought of a plan. He dropped his banana skin on the path. Perhaps the wolf would slip on it and hit his head on the big stone! Hiawatha scrambled up a tree to watch.

The wolf grinned when he came to the banana skin. "Huh!" he snarled. "Think I'm going to fall for that one?" He tossed the banana skin into the bushes, laughed loudly and bounded forward. "YOW!" He stubbed all four toes on the big stone. SPLASH!

Little Hiawatha, safely hidden in the tree, laughed and laughed as the angry wolf hauled himself out of the pond and slunk away home to dry his dripping fur. Then, when he was sure his enemy was safely out of the way, he came down from the tree. He *did* enjoy his swim that morning!

Spring Tonic

"Come along, Roo," said Kanga. "Time for your Spring Tonic."

"Don't want it," muttered Roo.

"Yes, you do," insisted Kanga. "You want to be big and strong when you grow up, don't you?"

"No," said Roo.

"*What?*" Kanga was scandalized. "Of *course* you do. Now, come along!"

She held out the glass containing the Spring Tonic mixture, and at that moment there was a knock at the door.

"Bother!" said Kanga. She handed Roo the glass and told him sternly, "I want that glass empty when I come back!" Then she went to the door. It was Rabbit, full of news about the Flower Show.

"It's going to be a *very good* Flower Show, Kanga," he said importantly, "and everyone must enter something—a potted plant or a bunch of flowers or some vegetables. I'm entering carrots."

"Yes," said Kanga, "I'll enter something. Can't stay now, Rabbit. Bye, bye." And she hurried back to Roo, who was looking very smug. The glass was empty. "*There's* a good boy!" beamed Kanga.

Somehow, after that, Roo always managed to be alone when it came to Spring Tonic mixture time. "The kettle's boiling!" he would say, or, "What's that burning?" Kanga would rush off to see, and when she came back the glass would be empty.

The potted plant in Roo's nursery grew amazingly big, with flowers on it the size of teacups, and Kanga entered it for the Flower Show. It was much bigger and stronger than anyone else's potted plant and it won first prize! Amid much clapping, Rabbit presented the prizes, with a special award to himself for carrots. Then he announced, "First prize for potted plants—Kanga!" When the applause died down, Rabbit said, "You must have fed your plant with some kind of Spring Tonic mixture, Kanga. What was it?"

At those words a nasty suspicion crossed Kanga's mind. She looked at Roo, who gazed innocently back, but held his breath. "No," Kanga decided, "he couldn't have! Just plain water, Rabbit!" she smiled, and Roo breathed again!

Bags of Scent!

"**B**uy my sweet violets!" called a flower seller. "Only ten cents a bunch!"

"Ten cents!" spluttered Uncle Scrooge. "For *flowers*? Robbery!"

"Ah, but smell how sweet they are," said the flower seller. "The scent alone is worth five cents."

"Rubbish!" snapped Scrooge—but as he walked home he thought, "I wonder if the scent *is* worth five cents? What a lovely way to make money!"

Madame Bonfamille: "Do you stop at the Savoy Hotel?" **Conductor:** "What, on my wages?"

As soon as he got in, Uncle Scrooge took some old paper bags from the shelf (he never threw a paper bag away) and rushed into the garden. He popped a paper bag over every scented flower he could find, left them there for five minutes, then took the bags off and tied them at the neck with bits of old string. (He never threw string away either.) Then he piled the bags together at the front gate with a notice above them—FLOWER SCENT 5¢ A BAG.

Uncle Scrooge watched from behind the net curtains. Everyone read his notice and most people laughed. Nobody bought any bags—but then Daisy Duck came along. She picked up a bag and sniffed it. "Don't do that!" yelled Scrooge, rushing out. "You'll use all the smell up!" Daisy tossed her head and walked away, and Scrooge went indoors again. Next time he came out his notice had been altered. It said, OLD PAPER BAGS 5¢ EACH!

And Uncle Scrooge rather thought it was in Daisy's handwriting!

Toadstools

Two of Princess Aurora's fairy godmothers, Flora and Fauna, were having an argument about who was the best at magic.

"Don't forget, dear," said Flora, "*I* was the one who gave the Queen's cat magic claws, so it cleared that plague of mice from the castle."

"That's *easy*!" sniffed Fauna. "What about the time I turned the wicked witch's fingers into sausages?"

"Actually," interrupted Merryweather, "you are both complete beginners. After all, *I* was the one who gave little Aurora a real live rainbow to play with. She could cuddle up in it, slide on it, wear it as a——"

"Oh, all *right*!" snapped her sisters. "You do go *on*, Merryweather. And anyway, we *thought* of the rainbow. All you had to do was gift wrap it."

"Huh!" Merryweather was affronted. "And who got it down from the sky, I'd like to know?"

The argument soon turned into a quarrel, sad to say, and each of the fairy godmothers began to think of turning the other two into something that didn't talk and couldn't answer back. Being such magic people, all

Robin Hood:
"What kind of shoes are made of banana skins?"
Friar Tuck:
"Slippers."

106

three of them thought of the same thing at the same moment. All three of them snatched up their magic wands and all three of them shouted at the same time, "I'll turn you into a toadstool!"

And in the next instant, three rather fat little pink toadstools, each with a magic wand beside it, sat silently in the grass.

Princess Aurora woke from her afternoon nap, yawned, stretched, and wondered where her fairy godmothers were. She began to look for them, but found no sign of them anywhere. They seemed to have vanished completely. Evening began to fall, and Aurora became worried. She wandered through the empty garden, almost in tears, but then she saw the three magic wands, lying beside some toadstools. She picked up the wands and cried, "Oh, I *do* wish my fairy godmothers were here!"

In a flash, Flora, Fauna and Merryweather stood beside her.

"Don't you ever go and leave me again!" scolded Aurora, trying not to smile.

"We won't, dear!" they promised. And they never did!

Dopey's Safe Place

Beagle Boy: "Have you seen a policeman round here?"
Clarabelle Cow: "No."
Beagle Boy: "Good. Stick 'em up!"

Snow White wanted to do the spring cleaning so she sent the seven dwarfs out for a picnic. They each had a packed lunch and a bottle of lemonade, and they were very excited.

Snow White kissed them all good-bye, little Dopey last of all. "Now, Dopey," she said quietly so that the others should not hear, "do take care of your picnic lunch. You know how often you lose things!" Dopey beamed. "It's quite safe!" he whispered back. "I put it in my hat! I *can't* lose it!" And they set out.

They found a nice grassy clearing for their picnic and Happy put the lemonade bottles in the stream to cool. Then they all unpacked their lunch—all except Dopey.

"Don't tell me," grumbled Grumpy. "You've lost your lunch."

"I had it safe," said Dopey, frowning with worry. "I know I did. Oh, where *did* I put it?"

"Never mind," sighed Doc. "Have one of my sandwiches."

"Oh, *thank* you," said Dopey gratefully. He sat down on the grass to eat the sandwich, but in a little while he got up again. "I think this grass is a bit damp," he said. "I want something to sit on."

"We didn't bring a rug," said Bashful, blushing.

"Sit on your—atishoo!—hat!" suggested Sneezy.

So Dopey took off his hat to sit on—and out fell his picnic lunch! The other dwarfs all groaned but Dopey smiled happily. "There you are!" he beamed. "I *told* you I had it safe! Aren't I a *clever* dwarf!"

<table>
<tr><td>

○ ○

1
May

</td></tr>
</table>

Three-Legged Race

Gyro Gearloose: "I've got water on the knee. What shall I do?" **Doctor:** "Wear rubber boots."

The March Hare was very proud of his long legs. "I run so fast," he boasted to the Mad Hatter and the Dormouse, "I could be at the Red Queen's palace before you were out of this garden." He kicked his long legs in the air nonchalantly—and tipped over the deck chair he was sitting in. "Ow!" he yelled. "My ankle! OW!"

His friends disentangled him from the deck chair and bandaged up his sprained ankle. "Oh," groaned the March Hare, "I shall have to walk with a stick. I'm crippled for life. O-ooh."

The Mad Hatter grinned. "I bet the Dormouse and I could reach the Red Queen's palace before you *now!*"

"Rubbish!" retorted the March Hare with a flash of his old spirit. "I'd take you on any time, stick or no stick." Then he thought a bit more and added, "But if I'm stuck with a stick, you should be stuck with each other. You and the Dormouse must tie yourselves together."

"A three-legged race," yawned the Dormouse.

"That's it!" agreed the March Hare enthusiastically. "Me with two legs and a stick and you with three legs between you."

And so they set off. The Mad Hatter and the Dormouse got on splendidly, striding out at a great rate. The poor March Hare, hobbling along with his stick, groaned to himself. "They'll be there *hours* before me! What a fool I'll look!"

He struggled on. A crowd gathered and shouted encouragement. "Come on, Hare! Don't be beaten!"

"I *am* beaten," moaned the March Hare. "And my ankle *does* hurt!"

But just before the palace gates he saw a strange sight. The Mad Hatter was shuffling along very slowly, supporting a completely limp Dormouse! The March Hare laughed. "The Dormouse has gone to sleep!" he shouted—and broke into a stick-and-one-foot gallop. He was laughing so loudly as he passed them that the Dormouse woke up and put on a burst of speed—but too late. The March Hare had won!

"I knew I'd win!" he said as the cheering died down. "Never doubted it for a moment!"

Clarabelle Cow:
"Must I stick this stamp on myself?"
Post Office Clerk:
"No, stick it on the envelope."

Dumbo Plays Cricket

One day when Dumbo was with the circus in London, he came across some boys playing cricket in the park. He stopped to watch. After a while one of the boys went home and then there was an argument because one side had more people in it than the other. "One of you ought to sit out," said the captain. "Or else we need another player."

"I'll play!" offered Dumbo. "I'd love to learn to play cricket!"

"Don't be silly!" giggled the boys. "Elephants can't play cricket!"

Dumbo felt rather hurt, but he just went on watching the game. Presently one of the boys took an enormous swipe at the ball. It soared into the air and landed on the roof of a house the other side of the railings.

"Six!" shouted the boy who had hit it.

"That's all very well," grumbled the others, "but how are we to get our ball back?"

"Knock at the door and ask!" said the boy cheerfully. So they went round to the house and knocked at the door.

An old lady came out and said, "I'm sorry, my dears, but you can't possibly have your ball back. Just look where it is—stuck beside the chimney pot! You don't think I can climb up there and get it, do you?"

"No," admitted the boys, crestfallen. "That's the end of our game, then."

They turned to go away, but Dumbo, who had followed them, suddenly said, "I can get your ball back for you!"

"*You* can?" The boys were amazed. "But elephants can't climb up houses!"

"They can fly!" smiled Dumbo. "At least, *I* can!" And he spread his enormous ears and soared into the air. Up over the roof he flew, neatly picking up the ball in his trunk as he zoomed past the chimney pot. With an expert flick, he tossed the ball to the captain, then flew back over the railings and landed beside the cricket pitch. The boys came running to meet him.

"That was great!" they shouted. "Elephants *can* play cricket! At least, *you* can!"

"Thank you," smiled Dumbo. He joined in the match and thoroughly enjoyed the rest of the afternoon!

Thomas Takes a Bow!

Thomas O'Malley, the alley cat, sat on the pavement and thought. How could he persuade Duchess, the beautiful Aristocat, to come out for a walk with him? She had been very standoffish lately and Edgar the butler had shouted, "Go away, you moth-eaten ragbag! No nice cat would be seen dead with you!"

Thomas sighed. He had washed himself all over several times, but he still didn't feel very smart. How could he brighten himself up?

A little girl came along with a doll buggy stuffed with pretty dolls. "Belinda needs a new hair ribbon," she complained. "This one's *two weeks* old!"

"Yes, darling, we'll buy her one," agreed her mother. They went into the shop, and in a flash Thomas was in the doll buggy. A smart ribbon around his neck was just what he needed! He pulled the red velvet bow off Belinda's hair and scuttled away with it. Luckily, the bow was elastic, so Thomas easily slipped it over his head. Using a shop window as a mirror, he straightened his bow proudly, then strode off to see Duchess.

"I have called to see Duchess," he said haughtily, when Edgar opened the door. Edgar stared at him doubtfully. "Er—is your name O'Malley—sir?" he asked.

"Certainly not," replied Thomas, pained. And when Duchess appeared he said with a wink, "A stroll in the park, my dear?"

"Delighted!" purred Duchess. Edgar bowed respectfully. "A pleasure to see you with such a smart gentleman, madam!"

"Thank you, my man!" said Thomas, and thought to himself, "It's amazing what a bit of ribbon can do!"

Honesty Pennies

Donald Duck was digging Daisy's garden. "Phew!" he gasped. "It is hard work!"

"We'll help you, Unca Donald!" offered his three nephews.

"You're not big enough," groaned Donald.

"What are these stiff plants with white pennies on them?" asked Huey.

"Those are called Honesty," said Daisy, coming out of the kitchen. "Now, what about some lunch?"

Huey, Dewey and Louie knew Donald would like to have Daisy to himself, so they offered to go and find a gardener. "What *kind* boys!" smiled Daisy.

But it wasn't easy. Everyone who liked gardening was already busy gardening. The ducklings were in despair —then Huey had a bright idea. "Pennies!" he said. The others looked blank. "Pennies!" repeated Huey. "On those plants called—er——" "Honesty!" said Louie. "What about them?"

"Uncle Scrooge!" chortled Huey, setting off at a run. "He'll do anything for a penny!"

Outside Uncle Scrooge's window Huey said loudly to Dewey, "Fancy Auntie Daisy's garden being full of pennies!"

"I wish *we* could dig it!" sighed Dewey with a wink.

"*Lucky* Unca Donald!" added Louie.

Uncle Scrooge was out of the house like a flash, spade in hand. When the ducklings reached Daisy's house half the garden was dug and Uncle Scrooge was still hard at it. When Donald and Daisy came out, the garden was all dug and Uncle Scrooge was very cross. "Where are the pennies?" he spluttered.

"Here!" said Daisy, picking some. "Honesty pennies for a kind deed!"

"Bah!" snarled Scrooge. "I never did like honesty!"

And he stumped off home, leaving everyone laughing.

115

Heffalumps and Honey

Kanga was collecting clothes for washing, and Roo was helping. "Sheets," counted Kanga, "towels, Roo's pajamas, Roo's bib—"

"And a heffalump!" shouted Roo. "A great big heffalump!"

"There's no such thing as a heffalump," said Kanga.

"There is!" Roo argued. "There's a heffalump chasing me and I'm going to hide!" He jumped into the laundry basket and pulled the sheets and towels over him—but Kanga had gone to get a pillowcase and didn't see him jump in the basket.

"M'm!" yawned Roo. "It's cozy in here!" He was so warm and comfortable that he fell fast asleep.

Kanga came back and whisked up a sinkful of soapsuds. "Rub-a-dub-dub," she sang. "Rub-a—come on, Roo, you sing too!"

But there was no answer. "Roo? Where are you?" called Kanga. "Oh, dear—perhaps there really *are* heffalumps! Suppose a heffalump has stolen Roo?"

Roo, hidden in the laundry basket, began to snore. "Help!" shrieked silly Kanga. "There's a heffalump in my laundry basket!"

Pluto: "How do you take a gorilla's temperature?"
Goofy: "Very carefully."

116

She rushed off to Pooh's house where he and Piglet were having a little something to eat. "There's a heffalump," she panted, "in my laundry basket. Help!"

Piglet turned pale. "I'm not very good with heffalumps," he squeaked.

Pooh put down his honey spoon regretfully and said, "I think we'd better find Christopher Robin."

So that's what they did.

"A heffalump, eh?" said Christopher Robin masterfully. "Let's have a look."

He led the way to Kanga's house and they all peeped in through the door. Roo had stopped snoring and all was quiet.

"Heffalump," shouted Christopher Robin loudly, "are you there?"

Roo woke up with a start. "Huh? What? Heffalump?" He wriggled about, trying to get free of the sheets and towels.

Kanga shrieked and Piglet closed his eyes. Pooh said, "I think I'd better be getting along." But Christopher Robin walked bravely up to the laundry basket and pulled the sheets aside.

Roo blinked. "Where's the heffalump?" he asked.

"You're the heffalump!" laughed Christopher Robin.

"A *dear* little heffalump!" cooed Kanga, hugging Roo.

"Time for a little something," said Pooh.

And they all went to help him finish his pot of honey.

Leaks and Leeks

The animals were holding a garden party. Minnie Mouse was organizing the egg and spoon race and Horace Horsecollar was running the 'Pin the Tail on the Donkey' stand. ("*Not* on the horse!" he said firmly.) Clarabelle Cow was raffling some thick cream and Daisy Duck was at the flower stall, selling house leeks.

"What are house leeks?" the animals wanted to know.

"They are little spiky plants, look," said Daisy. "A bit like cactuses but without prickles. I've got heaps of them at home. They spread so quickly, you know. You start with one or two and before you know where you are they're all over the place."

Donald Duck had come to the garden party and before long he made his way to Daisy's stall. To his annoyance, Gladstone Gander was there, leaning against the stall and chatting to Daisy. "House leeks spread so quickly," Daisy was saying. "I just had one or two at first and now they're all over the place."

Gus: "Have you heard? It's all over the building!"
Jaq: "Gosh, no, what is it?"
Gus: "The roof!"

118

"Funny things, aren't they!" agreed Gladstone cheerfully. Donald's eyes bulged. Poor, darling Daisy! Her house was leaking and that stupid gander did nothing about it except grin like an idiot! What Daisy needed was a man of action, not a nitwitted windbag like Gladstone! Muttering darkly to himself, Donald hurried to Daisy's house, stopping on the way to collect a ladder, some putty and a few tools.

Donald leaned his ladder against Daisy's roof, climbed up and started to crawl about on the tiles, looking for leaks. "Trouble is," he muttered, "you can't find a leak without water." He climbed down the ladder, filled a watering can and clambered up again. Then he poured the water over the roof, dangling upside down from the guttering and peering through the bedroom window.

"*Donald*," shouted Daisy, returning, "what *are* you doing?"

"Looking for house leaks," Donald shouted back.

"But they grow in the *garden!*" giggled Daisy. It took her a long time to explain the difference between leeks and leaks, but, as she said, "It was a kind thought, Donald." And, to his great joy, she asked him in for a cup of tea.

7

May

Walrus: "What is the best thing to put into a pork pie?"
Carpenter: "Teeth?"

Plenty of Soap

O ne day, when Peter Pan was dozing carelessly on the beach, the wicked pirate, Captain Hook, crept up and grabbed him. "Aha!" he snarled. "Got you at last!" And, wriggle as Peter might, he could not escape. Tied up like a Christmas parcel, he was flung into the bottom of the boat and rowed out to the pirate ship.

"Now," gloated Hook, "what useful task can I set you to, my cocky little whippersnapper? Ah, yes! You can scrub the deck. The crew's been cooking french fries, and it's horribly greasy. Use plenty of soap, boy!"

The grinning pirate watched Peter as he scrubbed dismally at the dirty, greasy deck. Peter racked his brains to think of a way of escape. He was in a tight spot, no doubt about it! Suddenly he heard a faint 'Tick—tick —tick—'. The crocodile was near the ship! Having swallowed the Captain's left hand some years ago, it was still waiting for its chance to swallow the rest of him! Peter glanced up to see if Hook had heard it, too, but the Captain merely roared, "Get on with it, lad! Plenty of soap!" No, he hadn't heard the crocodile.

120

Plenty of soap! That was it! Peter lathered the deck until it was as slippery as a skating rink. Then, with a lightning dive, he grabbed Captain Hook around the knees. The pirate's feet shot from under him on the soapy deck. "Aargh!" he bellowed, flailing about. "Beastly boy!" He tried to stab Peter with his murderous hook, but, quick as a flash, Peter jammed the cake of soap on it. Then a quick push sent the pirate skidding across the deck and under the rail—SPLASH!

'Tick—*tick*—TICK!' The crocodile saw its chance—but that was the last thing it saw. The water was so full of soapsuds that neither Hook nor the crocodile could see anything at all—and they certainly didn't notice when Peter dived into the clear water on the other side of the pirate ship and swam home across the lagoon, laughing all the way!

121

8
May

Leapfrog

Donald Duck's three nephews, Huey, Dewey and Louie, were playing leapfrog. It had been raining hard, so they played on the path where there were no puddles.

Donald came along, looking very pleased because he had Daisy with him. They stopped to watch the leapfrog game. "I used to be leapfrog champion when I was your age," boasted Donald.

"Oh, Donald, how wonderful!" murmured Daisy. "Do show me!"

"Right!" said Donald bossily. "Now, spread out, you boys. A jumper like me needs a *lot* more space."

"But, Unca Donald——" began Huey.

"There's a puddle——" went on Dewey.

"At the end of the path!" ended Louie.

But Donald wasn't listening. "Huey, right up at the end of the path. No, much farther—that's better! Dewey in the middle—good—and Louie at this end, so I can jump over one, two, three."

"But, Donald——" began Daisy.

"Now, Daisy," Donald interrupted, "go and stand down there by Huey at the end of the line where you'll get a good view. My last jump is always my best."

"But, Unca Donald——" wailed the ducklings.

"Quiet!" snapped Donald. "Now—ready!" He took a long run up, leaped over Louie, then over Dewey and last over Huey—and landed SPLASH! in a deep, muddy puddle right beside Daisy, plastering her with mud.

"I'll never go out with you again!" she shrieked.

The ducklings watched as Donald rushed after Daisy.

"The leapfrog champion is a very good long-distance runner, too!" they chortled.

122

The Diet

Thomas O'Malley decided to go on a diet. "I am getting too fat," he told himself. "Duchess will never like me if I'm fat."

So next morning Thomas had no breakfast. He felt very hungry but he thought, "Never mind. Duchess will think I am beautifully slim."

But, just then, a woman threw a piece of fish into the garbage can. Thomas *loved* fish. He snatched it out of the can and ate it up.

Some men who were mending the road had stopped for breakfast. "Here you are, puss!" said one—and threw Thomas almost *all* of a ham sandwich. Thomas ate that up, too. After all, it would be rude to refuse!

After that, everything seemed to come Thomas's way. A milkman had a bottle with the lid missing, so he shared the milk with Thomas. A woman left a sardine can with one sardine in it on the kitchen table where it obviously needed tidying up. And behind the fish-and-chip store there was a feast of cod fins and all the lovely crispy bits out of the chip fryer.

By the time Thomas reached Duchess's house, he was so stuffed with food that he could hardly walk. Duchess was sitting in the sun in her garden. "Good morning, Thomas!" she purred. "You *do* look nice and sleek! Have some cream?"

Thomas blinked in amazement. So Duchess *liked* him fat! "Thank you!" he beamed. "I'd love some!"

And that was the end of Thomas's diet!

123

Fishermen's Folly

"**W**ill you come fishing with me, Minnie?" asked Mickey Mouse.

"No, thanks!" frowned Minnie. "Fishing is boring." So Mickey set out alone with his rod and bait and folding stool.

Donald Duck called at Daisy's house, carrying *his* rod and bait and folding stool. "I'm going fishing," he smiled. "Like to come along?"

"No, thanks," sniffed Daisy. "Fishing is boring." So Donald set out alone.

When he reached the stream, Donald saw Mickey sitting on the other bank with his float already bobbing in the water. "Hallo!" called Donald, setting up his stool. "Not out with Minnie this afternoon?"

"She wouldn't come," said Mickey. "She doesn't really understand fishing."

"No," agreed Donald. "Daisy doesn't, either." He cast his line into the water and sat down to wait for a bite. Mickey, on the opposite bank, waited, too.

Suddenly they both leaped to their feet. "Got a fish!" they shouted, and both started to reel in their lines.

Alice: "What's black and white, and red all over?"
White Rabbit: "A newspaper!"

"Mine's a big one!" exclaimed Mickey.

"Mine, too!" spluttered Donald. "It feels *huge*!"

What neither of them knew was that their hooks had caught each other and their lines were tangled together. The harder Donald pulled, the more Mickey thought his fish was trying to get away. They both tugged and hauled, much too busy to notice that a boat was coming along the river. They wound in their lines so tight that the tangled lines came—*plop!*—to the top of the water, and for the first time the fishermen saw what had happened.

"Hallo, boys!" called a merry voice from the boat. "Having fun?" It was Daisy Duck, lounging elegantly with Minnie Mouse in a boat poled by Gladstone Gander, who raised his straw hat and sneered, "Good afternoon, landlubbers!" And in the next instant the front of the boat had caught the entangled lines and pulled Mickey and Donald—SPLASH!—into the water.

When they scrambled out, the boat was far away downstream.

"Ugh!" spluttered Donald. "*Girls!*"

"They'll never understand fishing," agreed Mickey. And because they were cold and wet they packed up and went for a nice warm lunch—at the fish-and-chip store!

125

Bacon and Eggs

"Goodness, I'm hungry!" said Peter Pan. "I've been swimming about in the lagoon all morning, making ticking noises to frighten Captain Hook."

"Oh, Peter!" giggled Wendy. "You are naughty! He'll think it's the crocodile after him!"

"That's right," agreed Peter. "But it's made me hungry. Let's have bacon and eggs—lots of bacon and lots of eggs."

"You go and wash your hands and I'll start cooking," said Wendy. But when she looked in the pantry she found that there was no bacon. Of course! The Lost Boys had finished it up for breakfast. And, to make things worse, they had taken hard-boiled eggs with them on a picnic lunch. No bacon and no eggs! Whatever could she do? Wendy was in despair. But just then John and Michael came in.

"Look!" crowed John, putting a huge fish on the table. "I've just caught it!"

"And I've picked all these wild raspberries!" boasted Michael.

"You *clever* boys!" exclaimed Wendy. "That's marvelous!"

And when Peter came down from washing his hands —which took him quite a time because he played games with the soap—lunch was on the table. There was crispy fried fish, a dish of french fries, and a bowl of red raspberries dusted with sugar and topped with cream.

"M'm!" said Peter. "Delicious!" And when lunch was over he sat back with a big smile. "That," he beamed, "was the nicest bacon and eggs I have ever eaten!"

Duck Magic

Princess Aurora was in bed with a cold. Merryweather, one of her fairy godmothers, came to see her. "Fresh air you need, my child," she said firmly, opening the window. "Mustn't coddle a cold. I'll be off now." And she flew out through the open window, absentmindedly leaving her magic wand on the windowsill.

Aurora leaned forward to shut the window, and saw some white ducks swimming on the moat below the castle. They seemed to enjoy themselves so much, ducking their beaks in the water and shaking their feathers, that Aurora smiled. "I wish *I* were a duck," she said. Her hand was on the magic wand as she spoke and in a trice she *was* a duck, swimming on the water with the others.

"Hallo!" said the ducks. "Where did you come from?"

"Up there," said Aurora, pointing with her yellow beak. The ducks shook their heads. "We don't go in for high flying ourselves. Leave that to the swifts and swallows. You staying long?"

"I don't know," said Aurora. And indeed she had no idea how she would get back. But she had a lovely afternoon swimming and playing with the ducks.

As evening fell she knew that Merryweather would soon come to read her a bedtime story. She must go. Spreading her wings, she took off from the water and flew up as hard as she could. Oh, it was difficult! At last she reached the windowsill. With one webbed foot on the magic wand, she quacked, "I wish I were Aurora!"—and she was!

"What are you doing out of bed, child?" asked Merryweather, arriving with a swish. "I—I feel much better," stammered Aurora. "Good," said Merryweather briskly. "It's the fresh air, you know. Now, into bed quickly, and I'll tell you a story."

When the story was over and Merryweather had gone (taking her magic wand with her this time), Aurora called sleepily, "Good night, ducks!"

"Good night!" quacked the ducks. "Come again soon!" And there was just enough magic left for Aurora to know what they meant.

"I will," she murmured—and fell fast asleep.

Impailed!

Wendy had been cleaning her underground home and she came up to empty her bucket of water. It was beautifully sunny outside, but suddenly a black shadow fell across Wendy's path.

"Captain Hook!" she gasped.

"Aha!" grinned the wicked pirate, "'tis I! Now, my pretty maid, you shall come and keep house for me and my merry crew!" And he swept Wendy up in his hook-ended arm.

"Peter!" screamed Wendy. "John! Michael! Help!" But all the boys were out treasure hunting in the lagoon, and the only person to hear Wendy's cries for help was little Tinker Bell.

Tiny though she was, Tinker Bell had the courage of a lion. She flew down and attacked Captain Hook's nose, kicking and scratching furiously.

"Aargh!" roared Hook, "wasps! I've been stung!" Tinker Bell flitted quickly to Hook's right ear and bit it hard. "Ow!" howled Hook. "Help!" He dropped Wendy, and rammed her bucket over his head to protect himself from the 'wasps'. Dirty water cascaded all over him. Waving his arms like a demented windmill, he staggered to the edge of the lagoon and plunged in.

Tinker Bell and Wendy laughed and laughed. Peter Pan and the boys came rushing back, having been warned by the Redskins that Hook was up to his tricks again.

"Wendy! Are you all right?" asked Peter.

"Yes, thanks to Tinker Bell!" said Wendy. And far across the lagoon they heard a clunk as Hook reached the pirate ship, bucket first!

130

Little Balls

Bambi came bounding through the forest one day to find his friend Thumper. "Come and see what I've found!" he said breathlessly. "Little balls! Lots of them!"

Thumper stared at his friend, puzzled. "What sort of little balls?" he asked.

"Very small little balls," said Bambi. "Gray ones. Come and see!"

He led Thumper back along the forest paths until they came to an open glade. "They were here," said Bambi, staring at the grass. "Where have they gone?"

"There are some acorns over here," said Thumper. "Is that what you meant?"

"*No*," said Bambi impatiently. "I know what acorns are. These were much smaller than acorns. They were near a stone."

"Which stone?" asked Thumper.

"It was a stone I turned over," said Bambi. "I was scratching up some nice tasty moss and the stone turned over and there were these little balls underneath."

Thumper began to laugh. "I think I know what you found," he said. "Let's turn over another stone."

Together the friends dug carefully at another stone. "There!" said Thumper as the stone rolled over. "Now look!" Bambi peered closely at the stone, but saw nothing except some little gray insects scuttling away. "*Those* aren't little balls!" he said.

"Ah, but try scratching at them with your hoof, like you did when you were scraping up moss," said Thumper. Bambi pawed at the insects—and they rolled themselves up tightly.

"Those are wood lice!" laughed Thumper.

But Bambi shook his head. "Perhaps they *were* wood-lice," he said. "But now they're little balls!"

131

Stuck Up!

"I'm going to make toffee," said Practical Pig one morning. "Who's going to help?"

"Not me," said his brother Fiddler. "That's a hot job."

"Much too sunny for toffee making," agreed Fifer —and off went the two lazy little pigs to play in the cool forest.

Practical Pig stirred his saucepan of sugar and butter and molasses until it was thick and bubbly. Then, very carefully, he poured the boiling-hot toffee into a tray to cool. "To save arguments," he said to himself, "I'll divide it into three equal bits, then we can each have our share." He took a knife and cut off a third of the still-warm toffee—then stopped. He heard shrieks from the forest, and scurrying footsteps. In through the door burst Fiddler and Fifer, and hard at their heels came the Big Bad Wolf, black and hairy and hungry for little pigs!

Fiddler and Fifer rushed into the broom cupboard and shut the door. "Come out!" growled the Big Bad Wolf, rattling the handle. "I'm HUNGRY!"

"Excuse me, Mr. Wolf," said Practical Pig bravely, "but would you like some——"

"Aah!" snarled the wolf, turning around. "*Another* pig! You'll do!"

"——some *toffee!*" finished Practical Pig—and as the wolf rushed at him he thrust a huge slab of toffee into the wolf's mouth!

"Unk!" snorted the Big Bad Wolf. "Grr-mmp!" His teeth were stuck together on the toffee and he couldn't open his mouth!

"Now off you go," said Practical Pig sternly, "and don't come bothering us again. Out!" And he hit the wolf—*clang!*—over the head with the toffee saucepan!

Fiddler and Fifer came out when they heard this, and helped drive the tongue-tied wolf into the forest.

"Is there any toffee left?" they asked when they came panting in.

"I'd only cut off my bit when the wolf came," said Practical Pig. "He ate yours!"

"But he didn't eat *us!*" said Fiddler.

"Thanks to you," added Fifer. And they looked so meek that Practical Pig relented, as he always did, and they shared the last bit of toffee.

Minnie Tidies Up

"I'm going to tidy up," announced Minnie Mouse, rolling up her sleeves. Mickey looked alarmed. "It all looks tidy enough to me," he said.

"Ah, but that's because everything's been pushed into the cupboard," argued Minnie. "The cupboard is *dreadfully* untidy."

"M'm," muttered Mickey. "I think I'll go out." And off he went.

Minnie opened the cupboard. Towels, dishcloths, pots of jam, a broken alarm clock, a flashlight that didn't work, a butterfly net, a screwdriver, three old hats, half a candle and last year's calendar fell out. Minnie put the towels and the dishcloths and the pots of jam back in the cupboard. Then she put last year's calendar in the wastepaper basket. But what should she do with everything else? Minnie wasn't sure. She tried on one of the old hats and gazed at herself in the mirror.

There was a bang at the back door and in came Clara Cluck. "Hallo," said Minnie. "I'm tidying up. This hat would be quite pretty if it had a new flower on it, don't you think?"

"Lovely!" agreed Clara. "*I've* got a nice flower on an old

Chip: "What has ten legs, a green body and lots of fuzz?"
Dale: "I don't know."
Chip: "I don't know either, but it's crawling up your neck."

hat. I'll run and get it." She bustled off and soon came back with a whole bagful of old hats. "Oh, gorgeous!" giggled Minnie. "This pink flower is beautiful! Or perhaps the yellow one?"

When Mickey came back the kitchen was piled high with old hats.

"Oh!" squawked Clara, "I must be off. Keep those hats if they're any use. Bye-bye!" She scurried out.

Minnie bundled the hats into the cupboard. "Here's my screwdriver!" cried Mickey. "And my butterfly net! This alarm clock just needs a new spring and the flashlight needs a new battery. Candles are useful . . . yes, we'll keep all this. Where's the calendar?"

"In the wastepaper basket," said Minnie. "It's last year's."

"It's got a nice picture on it," said Mickey, fishing out the calendar.

He pushed everything back into the cupboard together with the towels and dishcloths and pots of jam and the big pile of old hats. The door only just shut.

"There!" smiled Minnie. "That's much better! I do like a nice tidy cupboard!"

The Pirate's Ghost

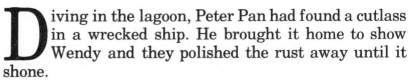

Diving in the lagoon, Peter Pan had found a cutlass in a wrecked ship. He brought it home to show Wendy and they polished the rust away until it shone.

"Look, it's got colored stones in the handle!" breathed Wendy. "Isn't it beautiful!"

Somebody else was looking at the cutlass, too. From his pirate ship in the lagoon, Captain Hook was staring through his telescope.

"Shiver me timbers! That's handsome!" he muttered. "Now, how can I get it from those pesky children?"

He thought of a plan. A little later, a boat landed near Peter's house and a large figure climbed out of it. Under one hook-ended arm it carried a white sheet which it draped over itself. Then it approached Peter's house, groaning loudly.

"Peter! Listen, someone's hurt!" cried Wendy. She looked out and saw a white figure. "I am the ghost of Long Jake," moaned the figure, "come for the cutlass you found today. Until it is back in my hand I can have no rest."

"Wait," faltered Wendy, terrified, "I'll get it." But she found Peter beside her, grinning. "Take this frying pan," he whispered. "I've got the yard broom. If it's a real ghost, it won't feel anything. If it's who I think it is, it'll serve him right! Come on!"

Then—Wham! Bang! Clang!

"Ow!" yelled Captain Hook from under the sheet. "Stop! Stop!" He ran to his boat and rowed away.

"Peter, however did you guess?" asked Wendy.

Peter laughed. "Ghosts don't have hooks!" he said.

136

Bubble Cars

Princess Aurora and her three Fairy Godmothers had been invited to a party at the castle in the sky.

They were very excited about it and spent a long time putting on their prettiest dresses and arranging their hair.

"Time we were off!" said Merryweather.

"How shall we get there?" asked Princess Aurora. "Are we going by magic coach?"

The Fairy Godmothers hadn't decided. "There's not much parking space up there," said Flora.

"No," agreed Fauna, "and the last magic coach I took had a *terribly* slow horse. I had to turn him into a dragon, and then he nearly set us on fire."

"Nasty," said Merryweather. "No, I think we'd better fly. Much the quickest." So she magicked a pair of wings for Aurora and they all set off, soaring up through the warm evening air. All went well until they came to a little cloud.

"It's raining!" cried Aurora.

"My hair!" moaned Flora.

"My dress!" groaned Fauna.

"My goodness," said Merryweather, "what a pickle!" She stared down through the sky—and saw a little girl blowing bubbles in her garden. "Just the thing!" she murmured. And—*ping!* In a trice, Aurora and her three Godmothers were each safely inside a huge, rainbow-colored bubble. Protected from wind and rain, they drifted upwards to the castle in the sky, where—*ping!* —the bubbles burst, and they were standing safely in the ballroom.

"How did you get here?" asked the guests.

"By bubble car," said Merryweather modestly. And nobody understood why Aurora giggled!

Cream Cheese

Thomas O'Malley:
"Where do you live?"
Scat Cat: "You see that large house way past those trash cans? Well, I live in the trash cans."

Wendy took a great pride in being a good little housewife. She planned all the meals a day ahead so that there was always something nice to eat. "Tomorrow we'll have rice pudding," she said. "There's lots of milk left over and it would be a dreadful shame to waste it."

But the weather was hot and thundery, and the milk went sour. "Oh, dear," lamented Wendy. "What a dreadful waste! Whatever shall I do?"

"Don't worry," Tinker Bell assured her. "There are lots of things to make with sour milk. Have you got a nice clean cloth?"

Wendy found a cloth and under Tinker Bell's instructions put it across a bowl and poured most of the milk into it. Then she gathered up the corners of the cloth and hung the dripping bundle over the bowl. Next morning the bundle had stopped dripping. "Tip it out into a clean bowl," instructed Tinker Bell. "Good. Now add some salt and pepper, and mash it in with a fork. Now you've got—"

"Cream cheese!" said Wendy delightedly. "But there's some sour milk left over that we didn't put into the cloth."

"That's for scones," said Tinker Bell. And, flashing about from cupboard to table, she showed Wendy how to mix flour and butter and sour milk into a light dough, then how to roll it out and bake it.

When the boys came in for lunch there were piping hot scones and helpings of fresh cream cheese. "M'm!" said Peter. "This is nicer than rice pudding!"

Evinrude the Rescuer

Madame Medusa was talking to Snoops on the telephone.

"Yes," she snarled, "we were cheated of our rightful prey last time by those nasty little mice who call themselves the Rescuers. But listen, Snoops—there's more treasure in our hidey-hole, and if we can just get hold of Penny again she can steal it for us. And this time there'll be no mistake!" She cackled wickedly.

Evinrude the dragonfly, who was hovering at the window, gasped with horror. He zoomed into the sky and hailed a passing seagull. "Quick!" he shouted. "Go to the United Nations building and get the Rescuers! And if you meet an albatross called Orville on the way, tell him Medusa's at it again!"

"Right," said the seagull, setting off. Evinrude rushed back to find Medusa still on the telephone. "On her way back from school?" she was saying. "In ten minutes from now? Brilliant, Snoops! The way I drive, I've got time to catch her." She slammed the telephone down and jumped to her feet. Preparing to go out, she glanced at herself in

the mirror, streaked on some more lipstick and ran her fingers through her hair.

Evinrude watched in an agony of suspense. The Rescuers would never make it in time! In five minutes Medusa would kidnap innocent little Penny on her way from school. Whatever could he do? Staring at Medusa's unruly hair, Evinrude had an idea. Women hated insects in their hair, didn't they? Right!

As Medusa came out Evinrude dived for her. His wide wings tangled in her hair, and she screamed and flapped at him, dropping her car keys. Evinrude saw his chance, disentangled himself, dived for the keys and clutched them in his four legs. They were terribly heavy, but he managed to drag them as far as a grating where they fell down—splash!—into the water far below. Medusa screamed with fury and tried to stamp on Evinrude, but just then Orville zoomed down with Bernard and Bianca, the Rescuers.

"Well done, Evinrude!" they shouted. "We'll take care of things now, but you've saved the day!"

The Penny and the Gun

"Just look at my spray gun," boasted Mickey Mouse. "It's so strong it'll make this green car red in no time. I'll go and fill it up."

Donald Duck's nephews, Huey, Dewey and Louie, saw Uncle Scrooge coming. "Quick!" they whispered. "Let's play a trick on him!"

When Uncle Scrooge arrived, the three ducklings were hunting about under the car. "A whole penny!" moaned Huey loudly. "Enough for a lollipop!" groaned Dewey. "*Lost!*" sighed Louie.

Uncle Scrooge stopped. "Lost a penny, have you?" he asked.

"Yes," sighed the ducklings, "and we're late for school. We'll have to *leave* it there."

They rushed off down the road, then doubled back behind the fence, to spy on Uncle Scrooge.

"A penny, eh!" chortled Uncle Scrooge. "Finders are keepers, they say." He bent down and looked under the car—and at that moment Donald Duck came along.

"Hallo, Uncle Scrooge," he said. "Lost something?"

"Nothing much," muttered Uncle Scrooge.

"Let's see," said Donald.

"No!" shrieked the ducklings from behind the fence. "Don't, Unca Donald!"

"Donald," snapped Uncle Scrooge, "your nephews should be at school. You attend to your affairs and I'll attend to mine." But Mickey had come back with the spray gun full of paint and just as Uncle Scrooge bent down, he switched it on. Whoo-oosh! Was Uncle Scrooge's face red!

"Bah!" he spluttered. "*Keep* your penny! I'm going home!"

When everyone had stopped laughing, Donald Duck looked under the car. "There's no penny!" chortled his nephews. "And there's no school, either. It's vacation!"

Bambi Gets Lost

Bambi found a butterfly resting on a bush. He touched it with his nose and it fluttered away just out of reach, looking as if it was going to settle again. It was a very pretty butterfly, with red and purple wings, and Bambi thought it was so beautiful that he followed it for miles, far away from his part of the forest.

It began to get dark, and the butterfly tucked itself away to sleep. Bambi stared round, suddenly alarmed. Where was he? A huge white face loomed down through the trees and said, "Too-whoo-oo!" Bambi shrank back in terror. "Don't be afraid," said the thing with the white face kindly. "I am an owl, and I can see in the dark. Why are you out so late?"

"I'm lost," said Bambi, "and I can't find my mother."

"I know where she is," said the owl. "Follow me." And he floated away into the darkness.

"I can't see you!" bleated Bambi.

The owl returned, blinking his big eyes. "That," he admitted, "is a problem. You daytime animals have such *silly* eyes. Ah! I know!" He vanished for a moment and returned with a lighning bug clutched in one foot. "*Now* you can follow me," he said.

Bambi followed the little light of the lightning bug safely through the forest until he was home. His mother *was* glad to see him. "Thank you, owl!" she called. But the owl had already gone, and all they heard was his distant call, "Too-whoo-oo"!

23
May

The Good Workers

Ludwig von Drake:
"Why did you leave
your last job?"
Jiminy Cricket:
"Illness—the boss
was sick of me!"

144

Minnie Mouse and Clarabelle Cow were chatting over the garden fence, taking a break from spring cleaning.

"What I say is," said Minnie, "if you want a job done properly, then it's up to us girls."

"That's right," agreed Clarabelle. "Boys talk a lot about what good workers they are, but they don't get on with the job."

"Take Mickey, now," said Minnie. "Always wanting to stop for a cup of tea. He's so lazy, it's a wonder the spiders don't spin cobwebs on him!"

Just then Mickey came up the path. "Cobwebs on whom?" he asked.

Minnie and Clarabelle giggled. "Er—on Grandad's portrait," said Minnie.

"Do you want a hand with the spring cleaning?" asked Mickey. "I'm very good at it, you know. Better than you girls!"

Minnie and Clarabelle nudged each other and giggled again. "You can clean the windows," said Minnie, "outside. Too many cobwebs inside!"

"I don't understand this joke about cobwebs," muttered Mickey. He got a bucket of water and started to

clean the windows, but he soon got tired of it. "Minnie!"
he called. "What about a cup of tea?" Clarabelle, hearing
this, gave a snort of amusement. Mickey glared at her.
"Minnie!" he called again. "Tea?"

He put his head in through the kitchen window to see
where Minnie was—and met a faceful of cobwebs from
Minnie's feather duster.

"Oh!" squealed Minnie. "Sorry, Mickey! Silly me!"

"Atchoo!" sneezed Mickey. "You don't *look* sorry! What
are you laughing about?"

"You really *do* look like Grandad's portrait!" giggled
Minnie. "Look!" She held an old picture frame round
Mickey's head and with white cobwebby eyebrows and a
white cobwebby beard, he looked exactly like Grandad!

"This cobweb joke has gone quite far enough!" sulked
Mickey—and he stalked off home to have a cup of tea in
his own house.

"There you are, you see!" said Minnie to Clarabelle.
"When it comes to work, boys are no good at all."

"Quite right, dear," agreed Clarabelle. "It's all up to us
girls."

And they spent the rest of the afternoon chatting over
the garden fence.

Smoke Signals

Pluto: "He told me he hadn't had a bite in three days—so I bit him."

Wendy was having a wash day. "How silly clothes are!" scoffed Peter Pan. "You should wear a suit of leaves, like me!" "Trousers are warmer," said Michael. "Not when they're wet," retorted Peter. "I'm going fishing. Good-bye!" And he flew away across the lagoon.

Michael frowned. "I wish my trousers *weren't* wet," he said. "I'd like to go fishing, too."

"I'll hang the washing by the camp fire," said Wendy. "It'll be dry in no time."

It was a windy day and the fire burned smokily. Wendy's washing, flapping on the line nearby, got in the way of the smoke and made it come up in puffs. The Redskins saw the puffs of smoke from their far-off camp. "Smoke signals!" said Tiger Lily. "What do they say?"

"It look like 'Come for lunch'," said a brave, "but him very bad signal. Not spell good."

"Never mind," said Tiger Lily. "I haven't been out to lunch for ages. Come along."

And so, just as Wendy was taking down the dry washing from the line, the Redskins arrived, waving tomahawks and yelling what Wendy thought were war-whoops. "Michael! John! We're being attacked!" she screamed. Tinker Bell flew off at once to find Peter, who was having a splendid afternoon's fishing. "I don't suppose the Redskins mean any harm," he said, pulling in another fish. "We're friends with them just now." But Tinker Bell tinkled so anxiously and whizzed round Peter's head so distractingly that he decided to go home. The Redskins were getting angry. "We want lunch!" they said. "She signal 'Come to lunch'—so where lunch?"

"Here lunch!" grinned Peter, unhitching his string of fish from his belt. And in no time everyone was squatting happily round the camp fire eating fish.

When at last the Redskins went home, Peter yawned and stretched. "You see?" he remarked. "If you wore leaves like me instead of silly clothes you wouldn't send smoke signals you didn't mean."

"But I'm glad they came!" cried Wendy. "It was *lovely*!"

"And anyway," said Michael sleepily, snug in his clean, dry clothes, "trousers *are* warmer!"

The Monster!

"Come along, Bambi," said his mother one day. "We're going to a new part of the forest where the grass is green and juicy."

"Can Thumper come, too?" asked the little fawn.

"Better not," said his mother. "If Thumper brings all his friends and relations our new place will soon be more crowded than this one!"

"But—" began Bambi.

"Come along!" insisted his mother.

It was quite a long way to the new part of the forest. Huge, dark trees loomed up to the sky, and a tangle of creepers almost blocked the path. Bambi felt rather nervous—especially as he thought he could hear a rustle of footsteps close behind them. Was it some strange monster? He stopped to listen—and the footsteps stopped, too. He ran on—and the footsteps hurried to catch up.

Stromboli: "Do you know if the bus runs on Sundays?" **Merlin:** "They usually run on wheels!"

148

"I can hear something," whimpered Bambi.

"Of course you can," agreed his mother. "The forest is full of little noises. Now, come along."

They set off again, and Bambi heard the footsteps scuttle along with them. He felt very frightened—but soon they came to a grassy clearing, bright with little flowers.

"Here we are!" said Bambi's mother.

"It's lovely!" exclaimed Bambi.

"Super!" chimed in a little voice. Bambi jumped with surprise, looked down and saw—his friend Thumper!

"I was lonely without you," explained the little rabbit, "so I came along. I didn't bring any friends or relations, though!"

"So *you* were the monster in the forest!" laughed Bambi.

"I'm not a monster," said Thumper modestly. "Just a rabbit!"

Pluto's Pigeon Pie

Pluto saw a picture of pigeon pie in Minnie's cook book. "Yummy!" he thought. "That looks good. How do you make it?"

"For this pie," he read, "take three fat pigeons." Aha! Pluto went into the garden to look for pigeons, and spied three lovely fat ones sitting in a tree. But how to get them down? Pluto scratched his head.

Suddenly one of the pigeons flew down, pecked up a long worm from the flower bed and flew up to the tree again. Pluto pricked up his ears. So pigeons liked worms, did they? He trotted indoors, found a long piece of string and took it into the garden. He arranged it carefully between two clumps of flowers, hoping it looked like a nice, tasty worm. Then he wriggled himself under a nearby bush, still holding the end of the string. He jiggled the string to make the 'worm' wriggle. When the pigeon came down for the string 'worm' he would jump on it! Pluto licked his lips, thinking of pigeon pie. He jiggled the string, and waited.

Up in the tree, the pigeons waited, too. Then one of them saw what he thought was a nice wriggly worm quite near a bush . . . He spread his wings, flew down and—peck!

"OW!" howled Pluto. "My TAIL!" He shot out from under the bush with the pigeon pecking fiercely at his skinny tail.

Minnie came out and shooed the pigeon off. "Whatever were you doing, Pluto?" she laughed.

"Making pigeon pie," muttered Pluto.

Minnie laughed even more and said, "I think the pigeon was making Pluto pie!"

150

Sawing and Snoring

The seven dwarfs were busy making a new table, measuring and sawing and hammering. Grumpy glared at Sleepy, who was doing nothing much, and said, "What a lazy dwarf you are!"

"No, I'm not," yawned Sleepy. "It's just that I don't know what to do."

"You could cut up some firewood," growled Grumpy. "Take some of those bits of wood and saw them up in the woodshed."

"All right," said Sleepy. He gathered up a big armful of wood, took a saw and went off to the woodshed. The other dwarfs joined planks together to make the table top and put a crisscross bit underneath to make it strong.

"Now for the legs!" said Happy.

"Where *are* the legs?" asked Doc.

"I don't know," said Dopey.

They hunted everywhere, but they couldn't find the legs for their new table. "They were on the floor," said Bashful, blushing as he always did.

Little Dopey suddenly had an idea. He rushed to the door of the woodshed and listened. Then he rushed back. "I know where the legs are!" he shouted. "Sleepy's sawed them up for firewood! Come and listen—you can hear him busy sawing!"

All the dwarfs followed Dopey to the woodshed. "Listen!" said Dopey. But Grumpy simply pushed the door open and walked in.

The sound Dopey had heard was not sawing but snoring! Sleepy lay fast asleep, the table legs untouched beside him.

"I got it wrong again!" sighed Dopey.

"Thank goodness you did!" beamed Happy. "Now we can finish our table!"

151

Lucky Pooh Bear

Christopher Robin was walking through the Forest when he heard some strange sounds: SLURP! "Mmmmmmm!" GULP! "Yummmmm!"

"That sounds to me like Winnie-the-Pooh eating honey," thought Christopher Robin.

Sure enough, Christopher Robin soon came upon Winnie-the-Pooh, who was sitting on the grass enjoying the very last drops of honey from a big honey jar.

"If I'd known you were coming, Christopher Robin, I might—I just *might*—have saved you a little honey."

"Thank you, Pooh," smiled Christopher Robin, "but I think I'm more interested in the jar than the honey, at the moment."

Christopher Robin looked at the empty honey jar very thoughtfully indeed.

"Christopher Robin," said Pooh, who looked thoughtful, too, "I am a bear of little brain, but even I know that you can't eat a honey jar!"

"Silly old Bear!" chuckled Christopher Robin. "I don't want to eat it! I want to *use* it!"

Winnie-the-Pooh thought that perhaps Christopher Robin wanted the jar for a hat—a rather sticky hat! But Christopher Robin explained that he had just been picking wild spring flowers in the Forest. He showed them to Pooh.

"I'm taking them home to Mother. I know she'll be

pleased, and I thought that if I could give her something to put them in, she'd be even more pleased. Your honey jar has given me an idea. It's just the very shape for a rather smart vase."

"A vase! A *vase!*" said Pooh. "Why, Christopher Robin—how clever!"

Pooh was so delighted by the idea that he hurried to a nearby stream to wash the jar for Christopher Robin. He left some water in it for the flowers. Christopher Robin put the flowers into it, and it looked really splendid.

"Er—if it would help you at all, Christopher Robin, I'll eat another jar of honey to make another vase for you to give to your Mother."

"Yes, please, Pooh!" called Christopher Robin. Then he hurried away to give the vase of flowers to his Mother.

Pooh Bear fetched another jar of honey from his pantry, so that he could empty it for Christopher Robin.

"Yum! Oh—YUM! What a delicious job to have!" munched Pooh. "Here I am—eating lovely honey, and helping Christopher Robin at the same time. Lucky old me! I wish I had an excuse to eat even more jars of honey!"

Can you guess what that greedy bear did next? He went to see his friend Kanga to ask if she would like a honey-jar vase for spring flowers. Kanga said she would, and so did Rabbit and Piglet. Even Eeyore the gloomy donkey said that a honey-jar vase might help to cheer him up just a very little bit.

Well, when Christopher Robin called for his second honey-jar vase, the next day, he found his friend Pooh looking very sticky indeed and surrounded by lots and lots of honey jars. His tummy was looking even more round than usual!

"Er—I'm helping my friends," said Pooh, between mouthfuls. "They all want honey-jar vases, you see, so I just HAVE to eat all the honey for them."

Christopher Robin couldn't help thinking that Pooh was being rather greedy, but then he was being kind as well, in a way, so Christopher Robin just smiled and said:

"Funny old Bear!"

Thomas O'Malley Goes Shopping

Duchess, the beautiful Aristocat, was out shopping with her three kittens, escorted, as always, by Edgar the butler.

Thomas O'Malley watched from behind a lamppost as Duchess went into a very expensive food shop. Catching sight of his reflection as she went through the plate glass door, Duchess turned and smiled at Thomas.

Thomas beamed. In a flash he was standing by the shop door, and when the next customer went in Thomas slipped in as well. Where was Duchess? Slinking cautiously past the cans of peacock livers, Thomas caught sight of her. Edgar was busy buying six dozen hummingbirds' eggs but he was still keeping a watchful eye on Duchess. Thomas decided on a bold approach. Purring loudly, he rubbed round Edgar's legs. "Oh, the dear pussy! Is he yours, sir?" asked the assistant. "What? Oh, drat it!" spluttered Edgar—and at that moment Thomas managed to trip him up completely. Edgar fell flat on his back in a huge pile of fresh cream pies, and Thomas, Duchess and the three kittens scampered away through the smoked salmon and the peaches in brandy, pausing only to snatch up a roast pheasant which they carried up the escalator and ate in peace and quiet on the roof garden.

Edgar, meanwhile, had been soothed and mopped up, and a search was started for the missing cats. At last Duchess and the kittens were found, washing their faces contentedly. And Thomas? Thomas was on his way home across the rooftops, after a thoroughly successful afternoon.

154

White Feathers

Clara Cluck gazed at herself in the mirror. "I'm tired of dreary old me," she sighed. "I'd like a change. Perhaps I could dye my feathers a new color. Or bleach them white. M'm—white would be pretty." And she went off to ask her friend Minnie Mouse how to bleach feathers white.

Minnie Mouse was not at home. The carpet was up and the curtains were down and the furniture was covered with dust sheets. "Looks as if Minnie is going to have the decorators in," observed Clara—and she sat down on a dust sheet-covered armchair to wait. The sun was very hot and the empty room was very quiet. Clara's head began to nod, and soon she was fast asleep.

Minnie came bustling back from the shops, laden with cans of paint. Mickey Mouse was with her, carrying a spray gun which he had offered to lend her. They stopped in the garden and put everything down. "It is kind of you to lend me the spray gun, Mickey," said Minnie, "but I don't know how it works."

"I'll work it for you," beamed Mickey. "You go indoors with the spray gun on its long pipe, and I'll see to the engine out here."

"But how do I do it?" asked Minnie.

"Just press the trigger and spray everything," said Mickey. "The furniture is covered up, and you want the whole room white, don't you?"

"Oh, yes," said Minnie, "I do." So Mickey started the engine, and Minnie went in and began to spray. It seemed so dark indoors after being out in the bright sun that she didn't notice Clara Cluck, fast asleep in the armchair. Soon Clara was as white as the walls.

"It works beautifully, Mickey!" shouted Minnie.

Clara woke with a start. "Eh? What? It's raining!" she squawked—and fled out of the house.

"Help!" yelled Minnie. "A ghost!"

The farmyard animals thought Clara was a ghost, too. "Help!" they shrieked, and ran away in fright. Poor Clara had to jump in the duckpond and wash the paint off.

"White feathers are all right for ducks," she shivered, "but not for me!"

155

Jungle Party

"I wish we could have a party," Mowgli said one day. Baloo looked puzzled. "What *is* a party?" he asked.

"It's when you ask all your friends to come," explained Mowgli. "You give them nice things to eat and drink and you put up decorations to make everything pretty, and you have music and dancing."

"So that is a party," said Baloo thoughtfully. "Goodness. Only the man-child could imagine such foolishness."

Mowgli sighed. "It was just an idea," he said.

That afternoon, when Baloo had gone, Mowgli walked through the jungle trying to find a friend to play with but there didn't seem to be anyone about. Bagheera was not stretched out along his tree branch and Kaa was not curled up on his warm stone. Even the monkeys were missing from the treetops. The whole jungle was quiet and empty.

"They've gone off to do something interesting," Mowgli said to himself crossly, "and they've left me out. How mean!" And, because there was nothing else to do, he stretched out in a patch of sunlight and went to sleep.

Much later, when it was beginning to get dark, Mowgli woke up. He could hear something strange—drums, and the chatter of voices. There was a good smell of cooking too, and strangest of all, a glimmer of light shone through the trees.

"Ah," said Baloo, arriving soft-footed beside Mowgli, "there you are, little one. We have a surprise for you. Come."

Mowgli trotted behind Baloo towards the lights and the good smell and the drums. When they arrived he gasped in amazement. Palm oil lamps in half coconut shells hung from the trees, and at one end of the clearing a monkey band played drums and maracas and bamboo pipes. Festoons of flowers hung everywhere and dishes of delicious food steamed temptingly.

"Is this a party, man-child?" enquired Baloo.

"It's a *wonderful* party!" beamed Mowgli. "But I thought you said my idea was foolish!"

"So it is," sighed Baloo. "But we all need a little

Donald Duck: "What is the difference between a jeweler and a jailer?"
Pluto: "One sells watches and the other watches cells!"

156

oolishness sometimes. Now, what is this thing you call
ancing?"

After that there was a little foolishness in the jungle
henever anyone felt like it, which was quite often!